D1553249

PRINCESS OF ESTORIA

DELANEY DIAMOND

GARDEN AVENUE PRESSS

Princess of Estoria by Delaney Diamond

Copyright © 2019, Delaney Diamond

Garden Avenue Press

Atlanta, Georgia

ISBN: 978-1-940636-93-1 (Ebook edition)

ISBN: 978-1-940636-94-8 (Paperback edition)

www.delaneydiamond.com

1

Prince Andres Luis Vasquez Alamanzar II of the Principality of Estoria eyed his older cousin, Juan the Viscount of Guzman, from his position beside him. They both sat in the opulent office of Prince Felipe, Andres's grandfather.

As the ruling head of state of Estoria, Felipe managed the country's affairs primarily from this office, decorated with dark wood walls and furnishings that consisted of a desk that was centuries old, and heavy wood chairs whose colors matched the room in maroons and deep brown. At the moment, he stood facing the window, listening to Andres and Juan debate each other.

"It's only a proposal," Juan said.

"A proposal that could annihilate the marine life that location is known for. It's the perfect viewing spot to see sharks, rays, and Eurasian otters. The eastern shore is one of the few tourism draws that we have in our country. If we disrupt that habitat, we risk losing animals."

As the outdoorsy type, Andres enjoyed horseback riding and water sports like kayaking and deep-sea fishing off the coast of the island country. The idea of harming or in any way disrupting the ecosystem turned his stomach.

He knew very well that his cousin Juan didn't care about nature and wildlife. The casino-hotel that he proposed bringing to the island would indeed generate additional revenue, but Andres believed the last thing they needed was another casino on an island that already had two—particularly one that could adversely impact the environment. In his opinion, the drawbacks outweighed the benefits. If he didn't know his cousin better, he'd think the man was getting a kickback.

But the truth was, Juan probably hadn't given the idea much thought and had been talked into it by his friend, one of the co-owners of the proposed casino. His cousin was simply not thorough. Because Juan was older and worked closely with Felipe on a number of palace projects, he was expected to take the throne after Felipe, but Andres had concerns. Hopefully, with the National Council for guidance, he would be a good ruler, though at times Andres questioned his judgment.

Felipe turned from the window where he had been looking out at the harbor. He wore a black suit and red tie. In his hand was a cup of coffee. Wrinkles lined his face, and the short hair on his head, as well as his mustache and goatee, were completely white. He looked, for lack of a better word, old, but in public maintained a certain vibrancy in appearance and walk. Only in private did he allow his shoulders to take on a gentle slope, like they did now.

"We should get the... What do you call that agency...? To look into it," Felipe said.

"The environmental commission," Andres supplied.

The commission was one of the smaller departments in the government, and depended on the state budget for a significant portion of its budget, much of which Andres had fought for upon his expanded role in Estoria's financial affairs a few years ago.

"Yes. Have they been contacted yet?" Felipe asked.

"Not yet," Juan admitted. "But—"

"Why not?" Felipe interrupted.

"My contact says we don't have much time. If they can't build here, the alternative is to take their business to Portugal. Do we really want to lose this opportunity to them?"

Andres gritted his teeth. Juan had purposely mentioned Portugal because of the contentious history between both countries.

Felipe's brows snapped together in concern. "Of course not. What do you think, Andres?"

"I think we should wait to do this right. The owners can't expect us to rush through such an important decision. If they do, we shouldn't do business with them."

Felipe nodded gravely and set down his coffee cup. "I agree. Here is what I suggest. Get me the proposal on the casino, and I'll look at it and be better able to make a decision at that time."

"The proposal was delivered to you a few days ago," Juan said with a frown. He pointed at the bound document on the desk.

Felipe glanced down. "Oh."

Andres frowned, too. The whole purpose of this meeting was to discuss the proposal and the potential for additional tax income from the erection of the new casino. Why hadn't his grandfather read the report yet? As a matter of fact, he seemed a bit out of sorts lately.

Andres stood. "I think we should bring this meeting to a close. Grandfather, you need time to review the report, and so do I." Much to his chagrin, he hadn't received a copy until today.

Juan's lips thinned into a line of displeasure, but he stood, too. "How long will this take, so I can get back to the owners? A few days?"

Andres shook his head. "I leave for the wedding in Zamibia day after tomorrow and won't be back until next week. Let's plan to meet when I get back."

He would read the report on the plane to get up to speed. In the meantime, he'd touch base with the environmental commission to get to work on a study on the impact the building and its infrastructure might have on the coastal habitat.

"Very well. Have a safe trip. Uncle, I await your decision on when we should meet again." Juan maintained a look of displeasure, but he nodded and exited the office.

As soon as the door clicked shut, Felipe said, "You don't like the idea."

"Not particularly. Aside from the fact that we don't need another casino, you know how I feel about preserving the environment and the animals we share this space with. There are other ways to make money, and we're currently doing a good job exploring them."

Estoria was a banking center with no income tax, low business taxes, and as a tax haven was on par with Malta in the number of offshore companies domiciled there. Its warm climate welcomed visitors all year round, and the rich and famous frequented its shores, coming over from mainland Europe to enjoy the weather and hide away in villas scattered throughout the country. At the same time, Andres and a team of advisors oversaw highly profitable investment portfolios and businesses here and abroad for The Crown.

"I trust your judgment. I'll look at the proposal while you're gone on your trip."

Andres picked up his copy from the edge of the desk and watched his grandfather settle into his chair.

"Are you all right, Grandfather?"

Felipe looked up. "Yes. Why?"

"You seem distracted of late. I just want to make sure you're fine."

Felipe waved his hand dismissively. "I'm fine. Don't worry about me. Nothing some extra rest won't help."

"Then make sure you get that rest," Andres said.

The old man smiled slightly. "I will. Enjoy your time at the wedding, and please give my regards to King Babatunde, Prince Kofi, and his new bride. I trust you've arranged a suitable gift?"

"Of course. For individual gifts, I chose a pearl necklace from the royal collection for the bride and engraved diamond cufflinks for the groom. As a couple, they'll receive a five-bedroom chalet in Switzerland with a stunning view of the Alps. Workers are getting it ready as we speak."

"Excellent. Then I will see when you return."

Andres bowed his head in deference and exited the office.

2

_____

S tanding on the balcony above the wedding reception of his best friend, Prince Kofi of Zamibia, Andres sipped champagne and kept his gaze glued to the ravishing woman seated at one of the tables, talking and laughing with other guests. Coming to the wedding, he hadn't expected to meet anyone. He'd simply planned to show up and then leave, but he hadn't been able to keep his eyes from Angela Lipscomb for more than a few minutes the entire night, and at one point her eyes had idled on him, too, suggesting that the interest was mutual.

The bride and groom had disappeared, with plans to leave for their honeymoon to Mozambique in the morning. Meanwhile, the party in the Great Hall continued unabated. Those who remained danced the night away to the beat of drums, drank Zamibian wine, and gorged on the wide range of food options laid out on the tables.

Angela wore a vibrant red halter dress that exposed her back, with a decorative neckline that looked like roses circled her throat. The dress banded around the waist and the hemline landed below her knees.

His eyes traced the length of her long dark hair and over the shape of her lips, down to her pointy chin. Her lipstick was long gone, revealing pink lips set against tawny-gold skin. He imagined her naked, spread across his bed and sighing with pleasure as he kissed his way down her abdomen.

Andres sipped from his glass.

He'd known plenty of lovely women in his lifetime and dated models and aristocrats who'd made sure that a surgeon's scalpel gave them perfect noses and breasts. Angela was lovely, too, but that's not all that drew his attention. There was more to her than that. She seemed carefree yet controlled. Funny yet serious. She fascinated him from a distance, and he was drawn to her, anxious to get to know her in a way he'd never been drawn to another woman.

His other best friend, Wasim, approached and stood next to him. Wasim was a prince from the Middle Eastern country of Barrakesch. He, Kofi, and Andres had been friends ever since their university days.

"What, or should I say who, has your attention?" Wasim asked.

Andres dragged his eyes away for a second to look at his friend. Wasim's dark eyes sparkled with amusement and the corner of his mouth quirked up in a knowing smile.

"Angela Lipscomb, the bride's best friend."

"Ah yes, Angela," Wasim remarked.

Andres watched him sideways, trying to ascertain his interest. He'd made a comment about her earlier. Was he also interested in the American woman?

"Are you interested?" he asked.

"She's beautiful, but no. My attention is elsewhere." Wasim spoke slowly, and Andres followed his friend's gaze to a petite woman with deep brown skin, spinning and gyrating her hips in the middle of the Moroccan belly dancers.

"Imani?" Andres asked, incredulous. He laughed and shook his head. "Kofi will kill you if you touch his cousin."

Wasim snorted. "Imani and I are friends. Besides, I didn't say I was interested in her."

"You didn't have to."

"Back to Angela," Wasim said pointedly. "Are you going to stare at her all night or do something about your infatuation?"

No way he was leaving without getting to know her better, and he was willing to ditch his security detail to do that. He grinned at his friend. "I'm going to do something."

ANGELA POPPED the last of a chocolate-dipped clementine into her mouth. She swayed to the music, watching dancers draped in traditional west African fabrics, with gold headpieces and their faces dusted with gold. They'd become the focus after the belly dancers took a break, and these performers entertained the guests by teaching them how to perform the unfamiliar dance moves.

"You should join them," a voice said next to her.

She stopped moving and stifled a smile at the sound of his voice—smooth, cultured, and every syllable laden with a Spanish accent. When she saw him earlier, she'd let him know of her interest by making eye contact and holding his gaze for a few seconds before looking away.

"I'm sorry, do I know you?" she asked.

"Not now, but you will. I'm…Andres Vasquez."

Dark-haired and tall, Andres was a striking man. He'd removed the jacket and tie from earlier and wore only the suit's dark slacks and stark white shirt, which showed off his athletic build to advantage. His angular face was marked by high cheekbones, and a scar that sliced through his left eyebrow made her curious about how he'd received it. His lips were full and sensuous-looking, and his eyes sparkled like blue waves in the ocean.

"Nice to meet you," she said.

"And you are…?"

She had the distinct impression that he already knew her name, but she answered anyway. "Angela Lipscomb, friend of the bride." She returned her attention to the dancers.

"So, do you plan to join them?" he asked.

Angela glanced sideways at him. "I don't have the right moves."

"I doubt that," he said slowly, his gaze lingering on her body. "But they are offering what amounts to a class here, so maybe you should join them so you could learn the steps."

"What makes you think I want to?"

"When I walked up, you were already moving to the beat."

"The music is hard to resist, but I'll leave those moves to everyone else," Angela replied.

After a few seconds of silence, he spoke again. "How do you like Zamibia?"

"I like it."

"Any plans to do some sightseeing?"

"Unfortunately, no. I barely managed to squeeze the time off from my job, so I'm flying back tomorrow. And you?"

"I've been here several times before. I know the country well because of my relationship with Kofi. Too bad you're not staying longer. I could have shown you around."

"That wouldn't have been necessary. Remember, I'm friends with the bride. Dahlia offered to arrange a guide and transportation in the country. I wish I could have taken advantage of it."

"Don't tell me you're going straight to bed as soon as you leave here." He arched the damaged eyebrow.

Angela laughed. "Unfortunately, yes."

"No, no. Have you even had a chance to explore the palace grounds?"

"Um…no." She hadn't done much of anything because of the wedding prep and spending time with her friend, talking as they caught up on current events in each other's lives. Then the actual ceremony and reception.

"Well, perhaps you would allow me to show you around."

He was nothing if not persistent. She liked a persistent man.

"So you're a tour guide?"

"Unofficially, yes." He paused. "You know, I've barely been able to take my eyes off you all day," he said, his voice lower, deeper. "Tell me, how can I spend time with you before you run away tomorrow?"

Her face heated at his words. From the corner of her eye, she saw that he continued to watch her.

"I'm flattered."

"You should be. That doesn't happen very often."

"What doesn't?" She twisted her head in his direction again.

"That a woman keeps my interest with no effort on her part."

"Oh my, you must be quite the playboy."

He chuckled. "Some would say so, yes."

"And a bit full of yourself, maybe?"

"A little." He held up his finger and thumb close together.

She laughed. "And what caused that, may I ask?"

"Growing up in an environment where I was given everything I want, whenever I want."

"Ugh. You're rich and entitled," Angela whined.

"You could say that."

Amusement in his eyes gave the distinct impression that he found her assessment humorous. Perhaps saying he was rich was an understatement. He looked like the type who came from old money. *Just how rich is he?* she wondered.

"In that case, I'll have to pass."

"No, no. Can I take it back? I'm rich, that's all. Forget the entitled part." He leaned closer. "I'm not giving up. I want to spend time with you."

Goodness, he smelled good, too. The spicy scent of cologne filled her nostrils. "Maybe you see me as a challenge…?" Angela whispered.

"No, that's not it." He looked boldly into her eyes.

"Then what is it?"

"Exactly what I said. I want to get to know you, spend time with you. Let me take you on an evening stroll around the property. No harm in that, am I right? You leave in the morning, and then we'll never see each other again."

Oddly, she didn't like the idea that they would never see each other again. And besides, what harm would a stroll around the property cause?

"No answer?" Andres prompted.

Angela took a deep breath. "Okay, I'll take you up on your offer. But no funny business."

"Funny business?" he repeated with a frown.

"That means, don't try to kiss me or do anything else outside what would be considered an act between friends."

He pursed his lips, ruminating on her rules of engagement. Then he smiled. "I will do my best. But I can't make you any promises."

3

"It's quieter back here," Angela said as they strolled side by side in one of the courtyards. She took a deep breath and inhaled the perfumed air from the roses in the greenhouses.

"Yes. Much quieter. Calmer. Peaceful," Andres said.

The royal family had opened the grounds in front of the palace so citizens could participate in the wedding festivities. Goats, sheep, and cows had been slaughtered, and fruits and vegetables harvested from the palace grounds for the three-day celebration. Traditional Zambian instruments played music that she could hear in the distance.

"You're not talking about this area alone."

Andres smiled ruefully. "No. This country in general is so peaceful. I can really relax when I come here. In my own country, I can sometimes feel stifled."

"And where is that?"

He paused. "Estoria. Are you familiar with it?"

"Vaguely," she admitted. "Most of my traveling for work tends to be to Asia. But Estoria…that's western Europe, right?"

"Right. It's an island country off the coast of Portugal. We have a little over one million inhabitants."

They nodded a greeting to the armed man and woman

standing guard on the property. Other guards stood in various places, keeping an eye on the grounds. They wore blue-on-blue military uniforms with a gun on one hip, a dagger on the other, and one hand on ceremonial spears at their sides.

Andres stopped and pointed at a looming dark land mass way in the distance. "That is Jaro Mountain. Perfect for hiking. There's a spot I've visited a few times where you can look out over the entire city of Jouba. You can see for miles. It's an amazing sight."

"Sounds lovely. I wish I could see it," Angela murmured.

"Would you like to? There's no reason why you can't."

"Tonight?"

"No better time than tonight. Since you leave tomorrow, correct?"

Angela bit her bottom lip and wondered if he was serious. "How far away is the mountain?"

"No more than a fifteen-minute drive. It's closer than it looks."

"Wouldn't we need mountain-climbing gear or something to get up there?"

"No, but do you have more comfortable shoes?"

Angela looked down at her shoes and shook her head. "I only brought heels on this trip since I knew I wouldn't be staying long."

"Don't worry. All we really need is transportation, and there is plenty of that. Kofi owns over a dozen vehicles, and one of them is a Jeep, which I've borrowed in the past when I visited."

"You must be on really good terms with him that he lets you borrow his vehicles."

He shrugged. "I've known him for a while. Come with me, and I'll show you the view."

"I don't know… are there wild animals up there, like mountain lions?"

He chuckled. "Not at all. But if there were, I would wrestle them with my bare hands to protect you."

She smiled. He was definitely charming. "Oh you would, would you?" She glanced at his hands. "Those hands look pretty smooth to me. They don't look like they've had much to do with wrestling or with any type of manual labor, for that matter."

He held up his hands and wiggled his fingers. "You'd be surprised the damage these smooth hands could do."

Huh. What did that mean? She arched an eyebrow and he laughed.

"So, do we go to Jaro Mountain?"

Angela took another look. Why not? "Okay, but only if you promise you'll protect me from any dangerous wild animals."

"You have nothing to fear when you're with me," he promised in a quiet voice.

He looked intently at her, and her throat went dry. He had a good sense of humor and a lazy, masculine grace, which she suspected was very misleading when coupled with those sharp blue eyes that studied her with unabashed interest. A sense of excitement filled the air, as if she'd stepped into an adventure that was only just beginning to unfold.

"In that case, let's go," she said.

Moments later, Andres drove them around to the garage in a golf cart. At the open entrance, several men dressed in military garb joked and chatted with each other. Inside, light illuminated a line of vehicles—SUVs, sports cars, and several Mercedes were lined up behind each other. The moment they saw the couple, they immediately became serious and stood stiffly with their arms held rigidly to their sides.

"*Ehk-aley.*" One of the men, who appeared to be in his early twenties, greeted them in Mbutu.

"*Ehk-aley,*" both Angela and Andres returned.

Andres said a few more words to the young man, and Angela had the distinct impression that he was talking about her when the guard shifted his gaze briefly to her and nodded.

Then Andres lapsed into English. "I would like to take this lovely woman for a drive. Is the Jeep available?"

"Yes, it is. Will you need a driver?" the man asked.

"Not tonight. We're going up to Jaro Mountain. We'll be back in a couple of hours."

The guard signaled to a second man, who disappeared down a ramp that led below ground.

"You speak fluent Mbutu?" Angela asked.

"Only a few words," Andres said modestly.

"Somehow I doubt that," she said softly, and he just smiled.

She envied multilingual people. The best she could do was memorize greetings and how to ask where the bathroom was in other languages. Numbers, logic, and interpreting facts was where she excelled, and the skillset served her well in her career as a management consultant.

A few minutes later, the guard reappeared driving a black Jeep and stopped in front of them. He exited and held the door open for Andres, while the first man opened the door for Angela.

"Thank you," she said, climbing in.

Andres took off down a tree-lined part of the property, exited through another guarded gate, and then rolled out onto the paved road.

As they cruised along, he opened the sunroof, and Angela gazed up at the star-spattered sky. She let her right hand dangle out the open window and allowed the cool breeze and the sounds of the night to enter. Soon, they were at the base of the mountain, and the Jeep handled the bumpy terrain well. After a short drive, Andres pulled onto a plateau and stopped.

"Are we there?" Angela looked around, but she mostly saw trees and bushes.

"Not yet." Andres exited the vehicle. He pulled a rolled blanket with a strap from the back and put it over his shoulder and then helped Angela from the Jeep.

She looked skeptically at the incline. "I'm not going to get very far in these shoes."

"We don't have far to go, but don't worry about that." Without warning, he swept her up in his arms.

"Whoa!" She closed her arms around his neck. "What are you doing? You can't carry me up the mountain."

"We're taking a well-worn path, but it can still be a bit treacherous, and I don't want you to damage your delicate feet."

Her heart raced out of control. "You're sure?"

He arched a brow at her.

"Fine."

He started the ascent and Angela relaxed in his arms. He smelled...amazing. That spicy scent invaded her nostrils again. Clean, fresh, and masculine. Her nipples tightened, and she curbed her initial desire to press her nose into the side of his neck or let her fingers play with the hair at his nape.

"Comfortable?" he asked.

"Yes," she whispered, finding it hard to speak.

"As I said, this is a well-worn path. Soon you'll see lamps lighting the way."

Sure enough, he banked a corner and a series of lights illuminated the ground, making it easier for them to see.

"Are these solar powered?" Angela asked.

"Yes. They charge during the day and light the path at night," Andres replied.

She could feel the muscles in his arms stretch and grow taut as he climbed up a craggy incline and bypassed a high, flat rock. They came to a patch of grass under a sprawling tree where a few more lamps were strategically placed. Though the walk didn't take long, he had to be in excellent physical shape to carry her that distance, and he wasn't even winded.

Angela dropped to the ground. "Thank you," she said.

She stepped carefully over to the edge and gasped at the view of Jouba before them.

"Great view, isn't it?" Andres smiled at her and spread out the blanket.

"Very nice," she admitted. "How in the world did you find this place?"

"A long time ago, when I participated in a charity hike with

Kofi. We climbed up the mountain and past the big rock. It was only when we were coming back that I noticed this spot because it's visible from higher up. Our group stayed for a while, resting, before continuing our descent. I made sure to memorize the path we'd traveled. Now every time I come back to Zamibia, this is one of my stops."

He sat down and leaned back on his hands. Angela removed her shoes and joined him, letting her gaze drift over the lights of the capital. The cool air brushed over her face and feet, while locusts and other night insects sang in the darkness around them.

Andres leaned toward her and pointed. "See over there? All that area used to be empty, but now it's filled with shops and commercial buildings. Over there is where they plan to build the new hospital. And there—" He leaned closer—so close she felt the warmth from his body and took the scent of him into her lungs again. "There is where they'll build a new football stadium. Or as you Americans say, soccer."

"Are you making fun of us?"

He reclined onto his elbows. "For not being more appreciative of the greatest sport in the world? Absolutely."

"Soccer is becoming more popular in the States. I live in Atlanta, and we have a Major League Soccer team now."

"Good for you. That's progress."

"I don't need your sarcasm." She shoved him in the ribs, and he caught her arm. For a split second, they stared into each other eyes before his fingers tightened right above her wrist and he pulled her down onto his chest.

Angela gasped and stared into his eyes. "What are you doing?"

"You know what I'm doing." He tucked a swathe of hair behind her ear and then smoothed his fingers down the length of the strands. His features tightened as his eyes followed the movement. "So tell me all about Angela Lipscomb," he said, his voice husky.

Her chest constricted at the way his tasty-looking mouth tilted up to the right. "What do you want to know?"

"Everything. Do you have brothers and sisters? Are your parents still alive? What do you do in Atlanta?"

Lying on top of him made thinking difficult. She couldn't help but notice the muscles that contoured his body and feel the erection that prodded her thigh, which she'd wedged between both of his.

She cleared her throat. "Both of my parents are still alive. I have an older half-sister, from my father's first marriage. I work as a management consultant for Myers-Gomez Consultants."

He folded an arm behind his head, while his free hand continued to roam, easing down her bare arm. He barely touched her, but his fingers felt as if they left the indelible mark of a branding iron.

"And you?" she asked.

"My parents divorced when I was nine, and I was raised by my paternal grandfather. My father lives in Spain and my mother lives in Italy with her new husband and two daughters."

"What kind of work do you do?" she asked.

"I'm in investments."

"That's nice and vague."

He only smiled.

"Is there are reason why you didn't go to live with either of your parents?"

"My grandfather forbade it."

"Forbade it?" she repeated, shocked.

"He's a very powerful man," Andres replied grimly.

She wanted to ask him more but figured she should shift the conversation. She let her fingernail gently scrape his left eyebrow, the one marred by the slanted scar that ran through it. "How did you get this?"

His eyes dropped away from hers, and he took her hand. "As a boy, I ran down the stairs, missed my footing, and fell head first."

Angela winced. "That sounds awful. I guess you learned your lesson after that?"

A cloud passed over his features. "I learned a lot of things that day."

She thought she saw pain in his eyes. "Andres—"

He lifted up with a swift motion and captured her mouth. She froze at the unexpected contact. Then her heart thumped against her sternum and she kissed him back. His fingers climbed under her dress, bunching up the fabric as he smoothed it up her thighs to the silky panties that covered her bottom.

Angela gasped, which gave his tongue the opportunity to intrude into her mouth. Andres sat up so that she was straddling his lap, and shoved her dress higher on her thighs. He kissed across her jaw and sucked on the side of her neck.

The bulk between his legs sent a signal to her spread thighs of just what he was capable of. Angela moaned, gliding her fingers deep into his thick hair and letting her head fall back to experience the full pleasure of his mouth's caress. Her eyes fastened on the star-sprinkled night sky, and she paused, suddenly caught in the snare of self-awareness.

What was she doing on this mountain, aching for a man she barely knew? Ready to let him do just about anything he wanted?

She pulled back and Andres stopped immediately.

"What is it? What's wrong?" he asked in a husky voice.

Angela swallowed and met his gaze. Up close, it felt as if his eyes swallowed her whole. "That was unexpected."

"Not for me. I have been obsessed with your mouth all night. Ever since I first laid eyes on you." His thumb traced her bottom lip and sent a thrill through her.

Angela dropped her forehead to his shoulder. "Andres…"

She wasn't opposed to a one-night stand but hadn't expected to have such an intense attraction to *this* man. Excitement thrummed in her veins, and she felt helpless in the face of such unruly emotion…out of control. What was happening to her?

He cupped her face with both hands and forced her to meet his gaze. A faint smile crossed his lips. "Don't worry. I will not ravish you on this mountain, no matter how tempting you are. Just allow me one more kiss," he whispered.

He kissed her again, harder this time. His mouth bruised hers with its intensity and he groaned when she flicked her tongue against his. When he pulled away, his breaths came in shallow pants.

"Perhaps we should stop now, before I forget the promise I just made."

Angela laughed shakily. "Good idea."

4

Angela and Andres spent another hour talking on the mountain. He sat leaning back on his hands, legs stretched out. She sat angled against him, legs curled to the side. Though the night wasn't cold, the warmth from his body provided additional comfort.

He seemed genuinely interested in learning more about her, and he was easy to talk to. She told him about her work as a senior consultant. The work was hard and the hours long, and she often had to travel, but despite the cons of her chosen career path, the greater pro was that she genuinely enjoyed the challenge of the work she did.

"Have you ever considered doing anything else?" he asked. His voice was a soft rumble in her ear.

Angela shrugged. "Not really. Consulting is all I've ever done, and it's the kind of fast-paced, demanding work that causes some people to burn out. I'm fortunate that I've even lasted this long. I like the high-octane pace."

They were quiet for a moment, listening to the night sounds.

"What kind of investments are you involved in? And don't give me another vague answer," Angela said.

"Yes, ma'am." He chuckled softly. "On my twenty-fifth birthday, I inherited a large sum of money and started a private equity firm. We have an office in the States. We provide financial backing for startup companies or those that need an infusion of cash for expansion, that kind of thing. I also run the companies that my family owns. We have holdings around the world—mutual funds, real estate, and commodities, to name a few—all of which I manage."

"Sounds complicated," Angela remarked.

"It can be," he admitted.

She had the distinct impression he was holding back, but why?

"Does your father or mother work for any of the companies?"

"No. Once my mother divorced my father, she wanted nothing else to do with our family or our businesses."

"And your father?"

"He and my grandfather had a falling out a long time ago."

"Is that why he lives in Spain and not Estoria?"

"Yes," Andres answered in a clipped voice.

"Oh." She sensed he didn't want to talk further.

They fell into a companionable silence and only the night creatures and the occasional distant honk of a car horn could be heard.

Angela stifled a yawn with her hand. "What time is it?" She didn't want to leave, but they couldn't stay out there forever.

She eased away from him so he could check his watch. He flicked his wrist and showed her the face of the Cartier timepiece dotted with diamonds.

"Oh crap! It's late. I have an early flight." Angela jumped to her feet.

"What time do you leave?" Andres stood more slowly.

"It's two o'clock in the morning and my flight leaves at eight. And it's going to be a long day because I have a layover in Spain before traveling on to Georgia."

At the time she had booked her flight, it had seemed like a good idea to leave the day after the wedding. Now she wished she'd been able to negotiate an extra day with her boss. Not only because she would be tired as hell when she returned to work on

Monday, but because she would have had more time with Andres.

She slipped on her shoes as he folded the blanket. This time, she refused to let him carry her and walked carefully down the incline, hanging on to his arm for support on the way back to the Jeep.

The ride back to the palace was silent as they both remained deep in their own thoughts. Regret tightened Angela's heart as she realized this was the last time she would see Andres.

She gave him a sidelong glance. Part of her wanted to spend the night with him. If only she didn't have to leave first thing in the morning!

They dropped off the Jeep and made their way by golf cart to the guest wing and took the elevator to the second floor where her room was located.

Angela stood outside the door, loath to say goodbye. "Thank you for showing me a part of Zamibia I wouldn't have seen otherwise. I had a nice time," she said quietly.

Andres braced a hand above the door, blocking the light in the hallway and casting a shadow over her smaller form. "I had a wonderful time with you, too."

She gazed up at him. "Thank you. Good night."

"Good night."

Neither of them moved.

"You're not leaving," she said.

"You're not asking me to leave."

"I should."

"Why?"

"I have a flight to catch in less than six hours." She sighed, and her heart ached all over again with the burden of saying goodbye.

Andres looked left and right down the quiet hall. "I have a suggestion. Why don't you stay up and sleep on the plane? Since my room is far, far away in another wing of the palace, I'll come in here and keep you company and make sure you don't fall asleep."

"Oh, really? How do you plan to keep me awake?"

"I have a few ideas." His gaze focused on her lips, and then he dipped his head and kissed her.

Angela pushed closer under the grinding force of desire and locked her arms around his neck. They pressed together as he wedged her between his hard body and the door.

He took the key from her hand and opened the door. They stepped inside, mouths still locked together in an all-consuming kiss. Andres backed her up to the bed and lowered her onto the mattress, his fingers tangling in her hair and his body settling over hers.

His wicked tongue stroked a line from the base of her throat up to her chin. She moaned as his moist lips sucked on her sensitive flesh. He whispered huskily to her in Spanish and filled his hands with her breasts, grinding his hips between her spread legs.

As hungry as she was for him, Angela yawned again.

Andres lifted his head. "This is not what usually happens when I'm in a woman's bedroom."

"I'm sorry," she whispered. "Don't stop. I really want to."

"You're tired," he said with a concerned frown.

"No, I want you." She cupped his face and lifted her head to kiss him, but he dodged her mouth and raised himself higher.

"I have no doubt that you do, but you're also tired. As much as I want you, you're not in a position to make love, and I don't know if my pride could handle if you fell asleep on me in the middle of making love."

"That would never happen, I'm sure." As if to prove her wrong, another yawn swelled and released and she covered her mouth, embarrassed and frustrated.

Andres stood and looked down at her. "Nonetheless, I believe it's better if we stop. There is no rush."

"I leave in less than six hours," Angela reminded him, standing, too. She almost reached for him, almost begged him to stay. Only pride kept her silent.

"Why don't you get some sleep. You have an early flight tomorrow, but if you don't mind, I'd like to spend the night anyway. No funny business." A humorous glint entered his eyes.

Angela barely gave herself time to consider his suggestion. "Okay."

A lamp beside the bed cast a warm glow on the white, down-turned sheets sprinkled with rose petals. They moved quietly. Angela removed her shoes and Andres took off his shoes and socks.

They climbed into bed and he pulled the covers over them. Stifling another yawn with the back of her hand, Angela rested her head on his shoulder.

"I don't think I've ever done this before," she said.

"Me, either," Andres admitted.

She gazed up him. "So why now? Why are you lying in bed with me like this?"

"Because you make me feel what I've never felt before, and now I'm doing what I've never done."

He said the words she hadn't been able to articulate. She wanted to sleep with him, but lying with him dulled the disappointment and allowed her to savor the time they had left in a different way.

She closed her eyes.

"Good night, Angela," he said softly. He kissed the top of her head.

"Good night, Andres."

ANGELA STUDIED her face in the bathroom mirror. No makeup today. She'd remain au naturale for the journey home.

She didn't look too bad, considering the long day yesterday and having gotten only four hours of sleep. She'd woken up early this morning, and while Andres slept she packed and changed into jeans and a loose-fitting shirt.

With a heavy heart, she scooped her hair into a ponytail and secured it with an elastic band. She checked the time on her phone and sighed. Twenty-five minutes until goodbye. The ache returned. The longing for something more.

A car would soon arrive to take her to the airport, and she and Andres would have to say their goodbyes. Maybe they could keep in touch? She shook her head at the ridiculous thought. He lived in Estoria and she lived in the United States. There was an entire ocean between them. In terms of long-distance relationships, living on two different continents didn't bode well for establishing a bond.

Curious about the country, she picked up the phone and entered *Estoria* in the Google search bar. She perused the details of the small country, scanned the online pictures, and scoured their page on tourism. Summer was when they received the most visitors, but they were known as a tax haven and playground for the rich and famous.

They were considered a rogue principality and had an interesting history. According to legend, a group of landowners and other citizens, tired of the taxes imposed by the Portuguese king, fled to Estoria—an unoccupied island twenty miles offshore. Much to the chagrin of the king, they established their own country on the land mass previously claimed by Portugal, and built a fortress-like palace on a hill from where they could defend it at all cost.

They eventually formed an alliance with Spain and adopted their language and much of their culture. While Estoria had formed additional alliances over the years, they continued to have a special bond with the Spanish, while tensions between them and Portugal continued to this day.

Estoria's head of state was Prince Felipe Luis Vasquez Alamanzar.

Angela frowned and looked closer at the name. Vasquez? Surely… No. Vasquez was a common name.

Quickly, she typed in the name Andres Vazquez and added Estoria. What she saw made her eyes widen in shock. Andres was not simply some wealthy European from old money. His lineage went back centuries, because he was none other than the grandson of Prince Felipe. He was a goddamn *prince*!

"Oh my god," she whispered. Why did he keep such important information from her?

Now she understood why he'd had that conversation in Mbutu with the guard at the garage last night. Since Andres was such good friends with Kofi, the young man was probably familiar with him and he'd asked him not to say anything about who he was.

She rushed from the bathroom and found him sitting on the side of the bed, pulling on his second shoe. When he saw her, he smiled sleepily and ran a hand through his lustrous hair.

"Good morning. How much time do you have?" he asked.

"You're a prince," Angela spat.

The sleepy smile left his face. "I was going to tell you."

"When?" she demanded.

She looked into his eyes. She wanted to articulate her concerns but knew he wouldn't understand. She'd been here before, dating a man who was famous and well-known. It had been a disaster, and one she didn't want to relive.

He stood. "I can't explain, except that I liked that you didn't know who I was. I wanted to get to know you, and you wanted to get to know *me*—Andres, not Prince Andres."

"You were purposely vague."

"Yes, I was, but for a very good reason. Please, let me..." His brow furrowed. "I want to continue seeing you after we leave here. Let me fly you home on my private plane, and we could spend more time together. All you have to do is say the word. Are you open to the possibilities?"

She didn't want a relationship. At least, not with someone like him. She'd promised herself a long time ago that she would never date another man in the public eye, and she'd managed to keep that promise all these years. She especially could not imagine being involved with someone like Andres, open to international scrutiny at the level he must endure.

"No, I'm not open to the possibilities. I can't."

She marched over to her carry-on luggage, and he came up behind her.

"Angela, I'm sorry. I know I kept my identity a secret from you, but surely you can understand why I did."

She swung around on him. "And you'll have to understand why I can't take this—whatever it is between us—any further."

"Why not? I want to see you again."

"I don't date famous men."

He shot her a startled glance but quickly recovered. "Why not?"

"Because I don't want to be a public figure, and I know all too well that's the life I'd have to be willing to accept if I dated you. No thanks."

"Then we hide our relationship."

"And how would we do that?"

"Sometimes I manage to escape my life. I can wear a disguise."

She shook her head vehemently. "Still not interested."

"Then what do I need to do to convince you to give us a chance? We had a connection. You can't deny that."

Desperation laced his words, and though tempted, she couldn't succumb to the all-consuming need for a man she barely knew.

"I shouldn't have spent time with you alone. I shouldn't have let you spend the night. The truth is…the truth is, I-I'm seeing someone." That was a lie, but he didn't have to know that.

His eyes narrowed. "Who is he? Is it serious?"

Angela hoisted her bag from the floor. "That's none of your business."

"I'm afraid it is."

"Why?"

His jaw tightened. "Because I'm going to take you from him." He spoke with such confidence that at first she was stunned into silence.

"Excuse me?"

His eyes bored into hers—an intense blue gaze that suddenly

made her uneasy while her heart raced with unwelcome anticipation.

"Yes," he said, almost to himself. "I am not giving up. I will take you away from him."

"No, you won't."

A smile filtered across his lips. "Yes, I will." He dropped a kiss to her cheek and whispered, "Have a safe flight, *mi amor*. I'll be counting down the days until I see you again."

Her racing heart left her breathless. "You're so sure. What makes you think you'll see me again?"

His luscious mouth quirked into a deeper smile. "Because I always get what I want, Angela. And I want you."

5

"Stop lying!"

Laughing hysterically, Angela strode inside the expansive entryway of her workplace after lunch. Plenty of sunlight came in through the atrium ceiling and the windows and glass doors on three sides.

She leaned on the arm of her co-worker and fellow consultant, Livia, a buxom brunette.

"What's so funny?" asked Carl, the security guard, standing beside the guard desk and looking up from his clipboard. He was an older man, tall and burly, with coarse, curly hair interspersed with gray on his head and chin.

Angela stopped in front of him. "Carl, you don't want to know. Livia was giving me a rundown of her latest date, and as usual, it was hysterical."

"Don't be too hard on those young men, now," Carl said.

"You need to warn *them*. It's tough out here for women," Livia said.

"Hell, men too. I'm glad I'm already married and don't have to worry about running the streets anymore."

"You couldn't have been as bad as the men out here nowadays," Livia said, resting her hands on her ample hips.

"Wish I could say that was true, but I was a hellion back in the day. Right woman came along and slowed me down. Just know that you have to kiss a few frogs before you can find your prince." Carl winked.

At the word *prince*, Angela's smile wavered. Andres had reached out a few times since her return to the States, but she hadn't heard from him in weeks.

After a few more words to Carl, she and Livia made their way upstairs to the tenth floor where they worked for Myers-Gomez Consultants, a financial and management consulting firm that contracted with clients from all over the globe. The firm rented out the bottom six floors and occupied the top six.

"See you later," Livia called, as they stepped off the elevator and parted ways.

"Later," Angela called back.

The receptionist came barreling down the hall toward her and she slid out of the way.

"Sorry, babe! I just dropped off something in your office!" he called, hurrying by to catch the ringing phone at his desk.

Angela kept going down the carpeted hallway, waving to associates as she headed to her office. It wasn't a corner office, but it was one of the largest on the floor, given to her because of her seven years of work with the firm.

She pushed open the door and stopped short. The vibrant room, decorated in yellow, orange, and green, now included dark red because of the roses sitting on her glass desk.

She was used to receiving gifts from clients—concert and ball-game tickets, gold pens, fruit baskets, and once, even jewelry. Clients didn't mind splurging to show their appreciation for the work she did. Coupled with the quarterly bonuses, the gifts were nice perks that made a hellish, demanding job a little less unbearable.

Among all those gifts, she could count on one hand how many times she'd received flowers, and each time they'd been mixed bouquets. No one had ever sent red roses. Yet a glass vase wrapped with a red velvet bow and filled with red roses sat on her L-shaped desk.

She stepped between the two melon-colored guest chairs and lifted the card from the bouquet.

Five.

That's all it said. Nothing else. Yet she knew without a doubt that Andres sent them. A client would have included their name, and so would anyone she was dating—*if* she were dating. She'd assumed that he'd given up trying to reach her. Clearly he hadn't.

After hanging her purse on the coat rack in the corner, she sat down behind her desk and stared at the roses. It had to be Andres, but what did the number mean?

She bit her thumbnail and swiveled in her beige leather chair. *What did the number mean?*

ANGELA REMOVED her horn-rimmed glasses as she paced the floor in front of the window in her office, wearing a headset and nodding to the requests she received from the woman at the other end of the line.

She stopped moving. "Not a problem. I'll have my team prepare two proposals with both scenarios so you'll have a good understanding of what to expect, and we'll list the pros and cons of each. Keep in mind, whatever you choose, our people are available to help you every step of the way. We don't leave you hanging. We provide the follow-up training you'll need to roll out our recommendations to your staff."

The woman breathed a sigh of relief. "That sounds perfect. When can I expect the proposals?"

Angela set the glasses on her desk and glanced at her open calendar. "I'll have everything for by Monday afternoon. You'll receive an email with the link to a password-protected site for your firm. Once you receive the password, you'll be able to log in and review the options."

"Perfect. I'll let Mr. Clark know. Thank you very much for your assistance."

"My pleasure."

Angela tapped the *Off* button on the headset and sank into her chair.

She put her glasses back on and shook her wireless mouse, ideas already racing through her brain at the options available, when the door to her office was thrown open.

She jumped and stared as Livia burst in and slammed the door. Grinning broadly, she raced across the floor and squeezed between the two melon-colored guest chairs to plant her hands on Angela's desk. She glanced at the line of five vases filled with roses on the credenza. "More roses?"

"Yes." By the third day, she'd guessed what Andres was doing. Each card contained a number.

Five.

Four.

Three.

Two.

One.

A countdown of the days from her not-so-secret admirer.

"Any idea who's sending them?"

"Not yet," Angela lied.

"Okay, we'll get back to that. Did you hear?" Livia asked in an excited whisper.

Angela had never seen the buxom brunette behave this way— at least not at work. She was normally very stoic and professional within the halls of Myers-Gomez, but was known to cut loose during happy hour at any of the local bars.

"Hear what?"

"We have a new client. You're not going to believe who it is. Trust me, you'll never guess. Guess." The words came out in a rush and Livia looked ready to burst with the secret.

Angela pushed back her chair and crossed her legs, taking a good look at her friend. "But you just said I'd never—"

"Guess!"

Angela held back a laugh. She'd never seen her friend so amped up. "Would I be as excited as you?"

"Maybe, maybe not. Come on, guess." Livia bounced on her feet.

The beige chair squeaked when Angela leaned back. "I can't possibly guess. It could be anybody."

"Think outside the box."

Angela sighed. She had a million more important things to do than play guessing games. "Um…male or female?"

"Male."

"Okay…a former client coming back?"

Livia sighed with the theatrics of a D-list actor. "I said think outside the box."

"Why don't you just tell me and put me out of my misery?" Angela smiled sweetly—too sweetly.

"You're no fun." Livia pouted, but just as suddenly, her face cleared. She lowered her voice. "I'll give you a hint. He's a prince. Literally. An actual prince wants to talk to Edgar about contracting our services for his firm." Livia stepped back with a flourish, placed her hands on her hips, and waited for Angela's reaction.

She had none. She simply froze. "A prince? Who…which prince?" She worked hard to keep the emotion out of her voice.

"Have you ever heard of Prince Andres of Estoria? Oh em gee, he is gorgeous!" Livia sighed. "A few months ago, he was seen bodysurfing in Thailand with Martina Esposito, a pop star from Argentina. And now, he's here! He wants to contract with *our agency*, and he's coming here, *personally*. Can you believe it?"

Livia paid attention to all the gossip in the magazines and knew more about the private lives of celebrities and socialites than the entertainment reporters and bloggers. To call her a gossip follower would be unkind. She was so much more than that. She could write the entertainment columns and have a lucrative career doing so if she ever decided to leave her job as a consultant.

"Wow. Prince Andres, huh?" Not only had she heard of him, she'd kissed him.

"Yes!"

"How did you find out?"

"You know I'm tight with Edgar's admin. She told me all about the proposed meeting and asked if I knew about the prince. Which I do, of course! I got her up to speed on him and Estoria." Livia sighed dramatically. She gazed out the window behind Angela with a faraway look in her eyes. "I hope I get to meet him. I better go check my hair and makeup. One never knows when a prince will be looking for his princess. Toodles!" She grinned and rushed off, slamming the door behind her.

Meanwhile, butterflies charted a course to Angela's heart, flapping their wings in rapid succession. What exactly did Andres have planned?

ANGELA STRETCHED AND YAWNED. She'd worked through lunch by eating a tasteless sandwich purchased from the deli across the street. She clicked through files on her computer and wrote a few notes. She needed to call a contact in Vietnam, but because of the time difference, she'd send a message and should have a response by the time she returned to work in the morning.

Her desk phone rang.

"Hello?" she answered.

"Hey, Angela, glad I caught you at your desk." The voice of Edgar Myers, one of the owners of the company, came down the line. "We have an urgent situation, and I'm going to need your help, pronto."

"What's going on?"

"Come up to my office and bring something to write with."

"I'll be there in a few minutes."

Angela grabbed a notepad and pen and made her way down

the quiet hallway lined with awards and collages of happy clients from the United States and around the world.

She didn't run into anyone since most of the staff was gone because of the late hour. She took the elevator to the top floor and knocked briefly before entering Edgar's office.

"Hi, Edgar."

She hadn't seen him in a couple of days. He spent a lot of time behind closed doors or in off-site meetings, drumming up new clients.

"Have a seat." Standing behind his desk, he frowned at a file in his hand, not looking up.

His office was very different than hers and indicative of his position in the company. It was a corner office and had a dark leather chair, a glass desk, and dark guest chairs. The larger space accommodated a small conference table, and the color scheme was black and white.

Angela sat down in one of the chairs and crossed her legs.

Edgar snapped the file closed and looked at her. He smiled without showing any teeth. In the past few months, more gray had appeared at his temples, his rotund figure had grown smaller as he lost weight, and he appeared more tired than she'd ever seen him before. And she knew why.

They'd been hit with a bombshell earlier this year when his business partner, Raoul Gomez, had taken leave for cancer treatments. He still hadn't returned, and rumor had it that he might not. Raoul had been the sales guy and the one staff found easiest to talk to, while Edgar handled the finances. Now he filled both roles—working hard to keep morale up and the company on track.

He took a seat and ran his fingers through his dark hair. "We recently landed a high-profile client and he'll be here within the hour. Ever heard of Prince Andres of Estoria?"

"Um...vaguely," she answered, sitting up straighter.

His eyes narrowed slightly. "Vaguely, huh? He definitely knows about you. Matter of fact, he asked for you."

What? Silence, as Angela scrambled to recuperate from that bombshell.

"He did?"

"Yes. Said you were the only one he wanted to talk to." Edgar did his best to sound indifferent, but curiosity seeped through in his tone and the way he studied Angela.

She laughed. "I only met him once, at a wedding—the one I went to in Africa back in April."

"Well, he might not have made much of an impression on you, but you sure made an impression on him."

"Well, that's good news."

"It sure is. Excellent news, considering the shit we've seen the past few months. Pardon my French. We, you and I, need to meet with him when he gets here. We need to put together a rough presentation on how to boost morale to increase productivity in his company. Throw something together from one of the other presentations you've done over the years, and get some help putting it together."

"You want me to throw together a presentation in an hour?" The question came out more high-pitched than she'd intended.

Edgar raised an eyebrow. "The short notice can't be helped. His people didn't give us much of a heads up."

She adjusted the glasses on her nose. "This is extremely short notice. I don't know if—"

"Angela, you're one of my top consultants." Edgar leaned forward. "You know the situation we're in. Half the time I don't know if I'm coming or going, so I don't have time to negotiate on this. The fact that he asked for you is a good sign. It means this contract just fell into our laps, without me having to go out there and do what I hate—shake hands and kiss ass. Pardon my French." He sighed. "Look, I'm pretty sure we have this in the bag. Imagine being able to say that a prince used our consulting firm for his personal business. That'll be PR gold for years to come. By the way, the company is. . ." He checked his notes. "A. Vasquez International."

Angela couldn't deny getting the business of someone as high-profile as Andres was quite a coup, but she simply wasn't ready to face him on such short notice. She hadn't had time to prepare!

She forced a smile to her lips. "I understand. Of course you can count on me."

Angela left the office, jittery and nervous about the meeting ahead. Andres may have stated he was interested in contracting them for his company, but she knew the real reason he'd shown up in Atlanta and called their firm.

He'd come for her.

6

Angela walked across the carpeted floor of the conference room behind Edgar.

There was Andres, looking out at the street. Night after night images of him claimed space in her head, and now he was in her office. She slowly inhaled to calm her nerves.

He turned unhurriedly and looked right at her. The Earth stood still. Ripples of tension covered the space between them and caused her stride to falter.

"Hello, Edgar. Angela." His voice hit like a blow to the abs, tugging on her belly, simply by the way his accented voice said her name.

Dressed like he was—in a long-sleeved powder-blue shirt and dark slacks—no one would ever know he was a prince. He looked like any other man dressed in business-casual attire. A supervisor, perhaps, because of the haughty angle at which he held his head. Except she'd passed a burly bodyguard right outside the door, and in addition to a driver, there were at least two more guards waiting downstairs. She knew much more about him after doing some online research.

The men shook hands, but Angela hung back. She angled her

eyes away from Andres's penetrating gaze and paid attention to her boss.

"We're very pleased you chose our firm to address your management concerns," Edgar said.

"I feel as if I had very little choice in the matter. When I met Angela, she spoke so highly of your organization. I knew that she, and your firm, could provide exactly what I need."

He was a liar. Myers-Gomez was a great company, but she hadn't sung their praises. If anything, she complained about her workload.

"Glad to hear that. We pride ourselves on our excellent service and we hire the best consultants in the business. Angela is one of them, as you're aware." Edgar smiled at her.

"Yes, I'm very aware," Andres said.

"Well, let's get started. Have a seat, and I'll—"

Andres lifted a hand and stopped Edgar's words. "There is no need for a long, drawn-out sales pitch. I'm already certain that I want to hire the Myers-Gomez team. I'm not shopping around and getting additional quotes. I told you what I'm looking for, so why don't we save ourselves some time? Prepare the contract and I'll sign it."

Silence filled the room, and Edgar glanced at Angela.

What could he possibly be thinking right now? She wished she could read his mind. Sure, they had a prestigious new client, but it was painfully obvious by the way Andres didn't bother to take his gaze off her and by his swift willingness to sign on the dotted line —contract unseen—that there was more to her relationship with him than met the eye.

Edgar flashed a grin. "Sounds good to me. I'll get the contract, and I'll leave you in Angela's capable hands. If you have any questions while I'm gone, she can answer them."

Normally, as the subordinate, *she* would be the one to get the contract.

Edgar let his gaze shift between the two of them before he exited the room.

The minute the door shut behind her, Andres said, "I like the glasses. They're very sexy."

She glared at him. "Why did you contact my job?"

"How else was I to get your attention? You didn't return a single one of my calls," he said.

"You should take that as a hint."

"I'm not very good at taking hints."

She wanted to flee the room but couldn't move. He hadn't touched her, but he held her in place just the same, with dark blue eyes that didn't leave her face.

"You had no right to come to my job," she said tightly.

"I wanted to get your attention. I lasted five weeks before coming here, which I think is admirable."

"You could have found another way. I'm easy enough to find for a man with your resources. Why didn't you come to my house?"

"If I had done that, I would have scared you off. It would have been too much, yes? So I did the next best thing. I said I wanted your services, and by doing so, I knew you could not avoid me."

"Whatever you're planning won't work."

"I'm planning to hire your consulting firm. I need advice and recommendations on how to deal with the morale problem at A. Vasquez International. That's what you do, isn't it? Advise and recommend?" He arched a brow.

"You know exactly what I do." Angela placed her hands on her hips. "I'm supposed to believe you're here about management consulting? There are probably at least a dozen other firms you could contract with."

"But none of them have Angela Lipscomb on staff." His disarming smile almost melted her resolve, as well as her panties.

He came forward with graceful steps, and confidence oozed from his pores with each movement of his body. She held her breath, waiting for his next words.

"So, how is your nonexistent boyfriend?"

"My boyfriend is—"

"Don't lie again. We both know what you're about to say is not true."

She paused. "All right, fine. I don't have a boyfriend. Obviously I lied for a reason."

"Care to tell me what that reason is? I know it has nothing to do with our chemistry, because you can't deny, we have plenty."

No argument there. "I told you already."

"You don't date famous men."

"Yes."

He blew a frustrated gust of air through his nose. His eyes narrowed. "And what should I do? Forget about us and pretend that nothing happened in Zamibia? I—"

"Nothing happened in Zamibia—"

"I *can't* forget. I can't sleep most nights for thinking about you." Raw emotion vibrated in his voice. "You're in my blood, Angela."

Inexplicable pain wrenched her chest and she took a step back. "You shouldn't be here, Andres." She turned from him with a jerky movement and bumped her hip into the conference table. She winced at the pain.

He reached for her and then let his hand drop. "You act like you're afraid of me. Are you?" His voice sounded strangled.

Not in the way you think. "No." She rubbed her bruised hip. The tension was getting to her.

He gave her a speculative look. "You're still angry because I didn't tell you right away that I am a prince."

"A little detail you forgot."

"I was wrong." He edged closer. "Have dinner with me and explain your feelings. Go into detail about your anger. Then I can beg for your forgiveness and you can put me out of my misery."

Tempting. Very tempting. She shook her head against the dizzying seduction of his voice. "No."

Andres may not be very well known in the United States, but he was known throughout Europe. He lived under a microscope. She'd seen how chaotic the life of her friend Dahlia became even before she married Prince Kofi. She saw how the royal family of the UK was hounded by reporters and photographers everywhere they went. That was no life to live. She wanted no part of it.

Though she complained about her career often, she had a good-paying job, and no one knew about the stains in the fabric of her family background. There were no photographers lurking in the bushes and no reporters rewarded for digging up dirt.

She stepped backward, out of his orbit and the draining battle to lean into him. "If you want to do business with us, that's fine. Anything else is out of the question."

Andres studied her for a moment. A rueful smile lifted the corner of his mouth. "What's between us isn't over. You know it, and I know it. But for now we'll focus on the business at hand. How about dinner, to discuss your ideas? Not a date."

"You're sure about that?"

"Absolutely. We'll call it a meeting," he said with a disarming smile.

"To be clear, I don't date clients."

"That's very wise, but is that rule bendable at all?"

She wanted to laugh but felt she'd be better off being firm with him. She suspected the moment he sensed she was weakening, he'd press even harder and have her second-guessing her no-famous-men rule.

"No," she said archly.

"*Demasiado.* Too bad," he said with a disappointed frown.

She ignored his pitiful face. "Where would you like me to meet you?"

"I'll pick you up."

"I can meet you. This isn't a date."

"Nonetheless, allow me to be a gentleman and pick you up at your home."

Edgar chose that moment to reenter the room. "All right, I have the contract right here."

If he noticed the tension, he didn't let on. He handed the papers and a pen to Andres, who quickly reviewed the contract. Afterward, he took a seat and signed and initialed everywhere that

Edgar told him, set the pen on the table, and then came to his feet again.

"Looks like we're in business," Edgar said as they shook hands. "You can expect to hear from Angela by the middle of next week. She'll do some research and prepare a report with the first steps for you."

"Sounds good. Before you came in, Angela and I were having a conversation about my schedule. I have a lot of ground to cover while I'm here. I'm in meetings most of the day and have to take a trip to South America. Because of my hectic schedule, she agreed to meet me for dinner to share the report with me. I hope you can accommodate my schedule."

Smart. By roping in Edgar, he ensured she'd show up.

"We can accommodate you with no problem," Edgar assured him.

"Good." Andres looked at Angela. "I cannot wait to get started."

7

W ith the Bluetooth attached to her ear, Angela exited her car and waved at her elderly Black neighbor next door, Mr. Jefferson. As usual, the old man kept an eye on the neighborhood from the rocking chair on his porch. He nodded a greeting.

He was the oldest person on their block, a holdover who didn't sell when contractors bought up the homes, renovated them, and sold them to young professionals like herself. Other than Mr. Jefferson, Angela was the only person who lived alone. Everyone else had a roommate or was married.

They had exchanged numbers not too long after she moved in. If she didn't see him for a few days, she called to check on him, and he kept an eye on her place when she traveled. Every now and again she sat out on the porch with him and chatted for a bit.

"Do you have plans this evening?" Angela's mother, Tessa Lipscomb, asked in her ear.

Angela slung her messenger bag over her shoulder and pulled department store shopping bags from the back seat, loath to admit even to herself that after she went into the office, she'd spent the rest of Saturday afternoon hunting for a new outfit for her meeting with Andres next week. "No, I'm staying in and working on a big project that got dropped in my lap yesterday. I'm working on a project for A. Vasquez International, owned by Prince Andres of Estoria, a new client."

"A prince! Oh my!" her mother exclaimed.

"Yes, a prince. No big deal," Angela said, more as a way to tease her mother than any real belief that he really was no big deal. The fact that Andres had flown across the Atlantic Ocean and signed a contract to do business with her firm—all for the sole purpose of spending time with her—was a very big deal.

"Sure, no big deal. You're funny," her mother said dryly.

Angela shut the car door and walked as she talked. "We're meeting for dinner next week to review my preliminary recommendations."

"Dinner? Is that a business dinner or dinner-dinner?" Her mother's voice took on that hopeful tone it always did whenever Angela merely mentioned a man. Being her mother's only child, the pressure was on to produce a grandchild in a timely fashion.

"This is business-related. It's just dinner, Mom, not a date."

Tessa sighed. "All right, dear."

Angela smiled at the disappointment in her voice as she unlocked the front door. "What's the latest with you and Dad? Is he finally ready to do some of that traveling he promised you'd do?"

Her father, Martin Lipscomb, used to be a record executive and when her parents met, Tessa was a secretary at the same company but left after she married Angela's father. Though he was technically retired, Martin worked as a music consultant, helping companies with the strategic marketing and branding of their artists.

Tessa lowered her voice. "To be honest, I think he's still working because of you-know-who. He wants to be accessible to her, and continuing to work means he doesn't have to use his retirement income to help her out of her scrapes with the law. She's practically still a dependent, and she's here, by the way."

Angela flipped the light switch and stood on the threshold of her living room, to the right of the staircase that led up to her loft bedroom.

You-know-who was her half-sister, Rebecca.

"What's she doing there? Please tell me she's just visiting."

Her mother's sigh came through loud and clear. "She's temporarily staying in the spare bedroom. She got evicted from her apartment."

Angela groaned and sympathized with her mother's situation. Tessa had experienced the wrath and dysfunction of Rebecca Lipscomb since the beginning of her relationship with Martin.

"Mom, you have to put your foot down about this. She's a forty-three-year-old woman, and at some point, she has to get it together."

"Sweetie, it's not me, it's your father. You know that. To be honest, I don't want to even try to talk him into an alternative. That's his daughter, and he's determined to help her, no matter what. He blames himself for the way she turned out. He believes if he'd been in the home while she was growing up, she'd be in a better position now."

"That's bullshit."

"Watch your language, please."

"Sorry," Angela muttered. "How much longer will she milk that daddy-deserted-me excuse? I wish you weren't put in the position of having someone in your house you don't want there. She can't stand you."

"We both have that cross to bear."

"At least I don't have her in my personal space."

At forty-three years old, Rebecca was fourteen years older than Angela. Instead of being a doting older sister, she had considered Angela a thorn in her side even before she was born. The problems started when Rebecca referred to Tessa as "the Black woman who stole my daddy," when Tessa and Martin became serious and he introduced her to his daughter. Rebecca's acting out continued and accelerated after they married and Angela was born.

As a toddler, Angela adored her older sibling but soon became aware that not only was the feeling not mutual, Rebecca's jealousy caused her to express outright animosity on numerous occasions. So much so that Angela's parents never left her alone with Rebecca.

Her older sister's resentment only increased as Angela excelled in sports, dance, and academics. Since she couldn't compete in those areas, Rebecca found a new way to get attention—courting trouble. She'd been in and out of jail for various reasons over the years, which included such offenses as public drunkenness, forging checks, and fleeing the scene of an accident when she shouldn't have been driving on a suspended license. The sister that Angela had looked up to when she was younger she now avoided at all costs, and had for many years.

They only spoke occasionally when they ran into each other at her parents' house, and the conversations were always tense and stilted. She longed for a relationship with her sister but realized a long time ago it was better to keep her distance.

"Well, maybe she won't be here for too much longer," Tessa said.

"Last time she stayed for six months," Angela said.

"Please don't remind me. At least this time I was smart enough to hide all my jewelry so there shouldn't be any pieces that go missing and are never found again."

She heard the weariness in her mother's tone, and her heart ached with sympathy. "If you ever need to escape, you know you can come stay with me for a few days."

"I know, sweetie. Thank you. I better go. Your father will be home soon. I had him run to the store to pick up a few things for me. Keep me posted on Prince Charming, and you take care. Love you."

"Love you, too."

Angela hung up, thinking that maybe she should have a talk with her father, but then changed her mind. That wouldn't help. He was set in his ways and bound and determined to be responsible for a grown-ass woman who refused to take responsibility for herself.

She left her messenger bag on the wooden bench near the door and climbed the steps to the second floor. Her two-bedroom two-bath contemporary cottage was in the perfect location. She could walk to Candler Park or go jogging on the Atlanta BeltLine, an expansive redevelopment program that currently consisted of open trails and parks.

Her home was the right size for a single woman who lived minimally. Although the master bedroom downstairs had a walk-in closet, an en suite bathroom, and opened onto a newly refurbished deck, she had chosen to turn the loft upstairs into a bedroom and added a bathroom with a large stall. She adapted the wide open space into a relaxing escape with a sitting area and a minimalist white and gray color palette. Plenty of light came through the windows overlooking the back yard and the skylight embedded in the vaulted ceiling above the bed, all of which could be shuttered to close out the outside world.

She quickly changed into jogging pants and a long-sleeved shirt and made her way back downstairs. She walked across the cherrywood floors in the living room, past the alcove she used as an office, and went straight to the kitchen. In the refrigerator she found a Styrofoam container of leftover Chinese food from a couple of days ago and stuck it in the microwave. As the food heated, she tapped her fingers on the countertop, contemplating the situation with Andres.

She looked forward to seeing him again with way too much anticipation. The sight of him knotted her insides and made her long for his touch. Their kisses in Zamibia had haunted her nights, and she definitely wanted more. And he was charming, oh so charming, making him difficult to resist.

She'd have to work hard to control herself with him during their non-date.

8

ndres's chauffeured car pulled up outside Angela's quaint little cottage nestled between trees on either side that reached almost as high as the rooftop. Tonight he kept a low profile in a dark sedan instead of riding in a limo, but the ever-present black SUV with his bodyguards followed behind as usual.

"Wait a minute, Gustave," he said to his driver, before the Frenchman could exit and open the door.

Andres sat still for a minute, thinking. No matter what Angela said, this was a date, and he'd never put so much thought into his plans with a woman. He was the prince of his own goddamn country, and normally that was enough to impress anyone who met him. But Angela had him analyzing his every movement and jumping through hoops. He wanted to show her he was putting in the effort to woo her, but at the same time didn't want to overdo it.

He wanted her to enjoy his company as much as he enjoyed hers. She'd made him laugh with her witty comments and snarky tone, and he'd been very at ease in her presence. He longed to rekindle that feeling which suggested, among other things, that she was exactly the kind of woman he could envision spending the rest of his life with, *if* he were interested in a lifetime commitment.

Marriage hadn't been on his radar before Zamibia. He'd had relationships over the years, but they could be time-consuming, so he preferred casual flings with women who felt the same. With Angela, though, he didn't consider the cost of time and looked forward to seeing her on a regular basis.

Andres took a deep breath and exhaled through his mouth. "I'm ready."

Tall and well over six feet, the Frenchman climbed out of the car and opened the back door.

Andres walked the short distance from the curb to the front the house. Before he could ring the doorbell, Angela opened the door.

"Hi," she greeted him.

"Hello," Andres said, his heart fast-forwarding into a rib-thumping gallop. He reminded himself not to sweep her into his arms. He simply smiled. "You look lovely tonight. I hope you don't mind me saying that."

"Thank you," she said demurely.

No glasses tonight, and she wore tan slacks and a button-down blouse with sheer sleeves and paired the outfit with low-heeled, brown, pointy-toed shoes. Her makeup was simple—very little on her face and neutral lipstick, while her dark hair flowed freely past her shoulders, brushing against cheeks heightened with color.

She took a few steps into the house and picked up a blue folder from a wooden stool before rejoining him and closing the door. During those brief moments, he caught a glimpse of cherrywood floors and tastefully simple mid-century furniture.

"I'm ready," she said.

Andres followed her to the car, staring and trying hard not to charge her like a bull or grab her perfectly plump ass. He had a plan, and that plan was now set in motion. He simply had to be patient.

Because he kept his identity a secret from her, she felt betrayed. He wished he could go back in time and change the way he'd approached her or at least at some point during the night divulge his true identity. He couldn't go back in time, so tonight he intended to demonstrate he could be trusted and she didn't need to worry about being in the public eye.

She slid onto the leather seat, and he climbed in behind her. Gustave closed the door, and within seconds, they took off.

"Are we going to get any work done tonight?" Angela asked, crossing her legs.

His eyes followed the movement, which was sexy even with her legs entirely covered in tan slacks. "Absolutely. I'll review your initial report on the way to the restaurant, and we can discuss how to proceed."

She frowned. "That doesn't give us much time."

"We'll have plenty of time."

"Where are we going for dinner?"

"Have you ever heard of La Cocina Patagonia?"

Her frown deepened. "No, it doesn't ring a bell," she said slowly. "What part of town is it in?"

"South Beach."

Her eyes widened. "South Beach? As in Florida?"

Andres nodded. "I have a taste for Argentine cuisine, which the Patagonia serves. The food is excellent. It's one of my favorite restaurants and I know the owner." He'd chartered a plane because he wanted to keep a low profile, which was impossible to do if they took the Royal Plane of Estoria.

"South Beach. For dinner." Angela stared at him.

"Yes." He leaned closer, and her sweet perfume filled his nostrils. His muscles strained under the repressed urge to reach for her. "Relax, Angela. Once we're on the plane, we'll have a light snack and spend an hour and a half reviewing your plans. When we land, we'll have dinner and then return to Atlanta. You might get back a bit later than planned, but I promise, your carriage won't turn into a pumpkin."

"That's cute, but what if I had plans?"

"Do you?"

"No, but what if I did?"

"I would feel terrible." And he would. He wanted her to enjoy herself, not cause her stress.

"I get the feeling you're trying to make me see what I'm missing."

"Is it working?"

"A little." A faint smile lifted the corners of her mouth.

"A little? Then I have more work to do."

She smoothed a hand down her thigh. "I'm not used to these types of grand gestures."

"That's a shame. Maybe I can make grand gestures your norm."

One of her eyebrows arched higher. "You'd be setting the bar rather high."

"But that's the point, *mi amor*. I told you before that I want you, Angela. But if you choose not to pursue a relationship with me, I intend to make sure that every man who comes after me falls short. And then perhaps you'll finally admit how much better things would be with me."

She laughed quietly and shook her head. "You get an A for effort, that's for sure."

"Then I need to work harder. I want an A plus."

She laughed louder this time, and the fact that he'd amused her, enough to get a laugh, satisfied him immensely.

Before long, they were in the air, and the flight passed quickly as they reviewed the details of her proposal. Considering the short notice, she was very thorough, making good use of all the information he'd provided. By the time they landed, they'd agreed on a way forward and devised a plan to tackle the issues.

A CHAUFFEURED silver Mercedes-Benz picked up Andres and Angela at the airport and dropped them in front of the restaurant. The faint sounds of Latin music spilling from the front of another restaurant down the street could be heard as the car rolled away.

La Cocina Patagonia was located at the far end of Ocean Drive and took up most of the ground floor of the boutique hotel above it, also named Patagonia. The location rested on prime real estate but away from the night-time craziness of crowded sidewalks and slow-moving traffic that South Beach was known for. They walked through the hotel lobby and were greeted at the entrance to the restaurant by an older Hispanic male.

"Your Highness, it's good to have you here. It's been a long time," he said with a slight bow.

Andres extended his hand. "Too long," he agreed. Both men shook hands briskly.

The man turned his attention to Angela and clasped her hand in both of his. "I am Armando, the maître d'. It's a pleasure to meet you, Miss Lipscomb."

"Nice to meet you, too," Angela replied.

"Everything is prepared for you in one of the private dining rooms on the second floor." Armando signaled to a waiter standing off to the side. "Mario will take you to your room and take good care of you. If you need anything, you know how to reach me."

"Thank you," Andres said.

Mario walked over, a stocky man with coffee-colored skin and short-cropped hair. "*Buenas noches*, right this way," he said in accented English. He escorted them and two of Andres's body-guards to a flight of stairs that took them up to the next level. The room he led them into had a large window that looked out onto the strip and the darkness of the Atlantic Ocean in the distance.

They strolled inside while security remained outside the door.

"Is Esteban here tonight?" Andres asked.

"Yes, he asked us to tell him when you arrived. I will do that now and he should be here shortly." Mario disappeared.

"This is nice," Angela said, walking over to the table set for two.

Andres helped her into her chair and sat across from her. They perused the menu.

"What do you suggest? We came all this way, so you must have a favorite," Angela said.

"The steak, of course, since we're at an Argentine restaurant. Their ribeye is incredible and the sirloin succulent. You can't go wrong with either one. For dessert, I recommend their most popular dish, the chocolate mousse cake. It's served with Venezuelan gelato."

She closed the menu. "I've made my decision. The sirloin with potatoes and the chocolate mousse cake for dessert."

"Excellent choice. I'll have the same, but the ribeye." He set aside his menu, too.

She glanced out the window at the cars passing by on the street. "Coming here was a bit extravagant for a non-date, wasn't it?"

"I like to treat the people I do business with well."

"So if you were working with one of my male counterparts, you would do this—fly him to Miami for dinner at one of your favorite restaurants?" she asked.

"We might do something different, but yes, I would do my best to impress him."

"You hired me. I'm the one who should be trying to impress *you*."

"You've already impressed me," he said.

"Save your flattery. I'm not sleeping with you tonight, no matter how extravagant this non-date is or how many compliments you pay me."

"I assure you, I have no intention of trying to sleep with you. Sleep is the furthest thing from my mind."

Their eyes locked for a minute before a faint blush tinged her cheekbones. "I mean it. Nothing is going to happen between us."

He grinned. "So you keep telling me."

"What do you hope to accomplish tonight?" she asked.

Andres propped his elbow on the table and rubbed a finger along his full bottom lip. "I don't think I should tell you. It might scare you away." His body throbbed with awareness as he looked into her brown eyes.

She took a shaky breath and glanced down briefly. "You're very intense, you know that?"

"You have no idea how intense I can be."

They stared across the table at each other again.

"Andres! It's been a long time." Esteban Galiano entered the room, looking suave in a dark suit. Behind him, Mario followed with a bottle of wine.

Both Angela and Andres stood, and Andres gave his friend a brief hug. "It's been too long," he said.

He and the restaurateur had known each other for several years. Not too long ago, Esteban married a woman who was a sommelier and she now oversaw the purchase of wine and spirits for all his restaurants. Married life suited him. His attitude was better, and from all accounts he didn't work as long or hard as he used to.

Introductions were made, and Esteban looked at Angela with interest. "I don't believe we've met before," he said.

"I'm a consultant with a firm in Atlanta—Myers-Gomez."

"I see…so this is a business dinner?" He glanced at Andres.

"Yes," Angela answered.

Andres met his friend's gaze with amusement. Esteban was sharp and had probably figured out there was much more going on than a business dinner. "You're coming to the tournament in Estoria?" he asked.

Esteban shook his head regretfully, segueing with ease into the new conversation. "I have a prior engagement. But I already know the outcome," he said with a twinkle in his eye.

"If you think your countrymen will beat us, we're well-prepared this time." He turned to Angela. "We're talking about polo. Unfortunately, the Argentinians dominate the sport. Currently, all but two of the top professional players in the world are from there, and he never lets me forget it."

Esteban chuckled. "I'll be sure to get an update on the results. And hopefully, this time there will be no injuries."

"I hope," Andres agreed.

"I will leave you to your...business dinner. I'm taking care of a few things in the office, and then I'm heading home."

"Tell Sonia I said hello," Andres said.

"I will. It was very nice to meet you. Perhaps I will see you again sometime." Esteban squeezed Angela's hands between his and then exited the room.

Mario poured them each a glass of wine, took their orders, and then left.

"Injuries?" Angela asked.

"I've had a few mishaps." The sport of kings, as polo was called, caused major injuries to many a participant, himself included.

"Like what?"

He shrugged. "Dislocated shoulder, broken bones, hand lacerations. Polo is physically demanding and there can be some serious injuries as a result of what happens on the field. I've seen men knocked unconscious after falling from their horse or accidentally getting hit by one of the mallets."

Her eyes widened. "I had no idea the sport was so dangerous. Why in the world does anybody play?"

"Why do people box, or waterski, or drive race cars? Injuries are part of many sports. In the case of polo, I participate because it's exciting, for the rush of adrenaline. Being one with the horse— one unit, working toward a goal is...it's hard to explain if you've never experienced it. I'm in an exhibition game before a charity tournament in a couple of months. That's what Esteban and I were talking about. You should come see me play."

"We'll see," Angela said, spreading the cloth napkin across her lap.

"Good."

"I didn't say yes."

"You didn't say no, either."

She shook her head in amusement and lifted the glass of wine to her lips.

9

A ngela walked along the beach, letting her toes sink into the cool sand. Andres walked beside her, sleeves rolled up and holding a bottle of wine in his right hand. His security team trailed them at a discreet distance. One of the men, a wiry blond named Ollie, formerly with MI6, carried her shoes for her.

Dinner had been delicious, as expected. The steak was tender and flavorful, the Malbec robust, and after dessert, Angela understood why the chocolate mousse cake was the most popular dessert on the menu, without having to taste any of the others.

After dinner, she—not Andres—suggested a stroll along the beach, to walk off the rich and delicious food. Her suggestion had simply been a ruse. She wanted to spend more time with him. His nearness teased her with possibilities, and like the first night they met, she found herself smiling and laughing often. But he was a little different tonight, too. Still playful, but more…predatory, and the way his eyes lowered as he assessed her appearance made her skin tingle.

She watched his mouth all night, aching for another taste of his lips and imagining for one second what he'd do if she bared her breasts to him. How his mouth would cover her nipples and his tongue would tease relentlessly until she begged him to stop.

"They fine you for having open containers on the beach," Angela pointed out.

"How much?" Andres asked, tipping his head back and taking a swallow. He looked very much like a vagabond—elegant but rough. Princely, yet with a wildness that simmered beneath the surface. In that moment he appeared as uncultured as his ancestors. Rude. Untamed. But utterly irresistible.

"I'm not sure. Fifty dollars. Maybe a hundred."

Andres shrugged. "I'll take my chances," he said.

Right away she realized how ridiculous her warning sounded. He could either flash his diplomatic credentials or pay the measly fine.

He stopped walking and stared out at the waves rolling in against the shore. Other people strolled the beach as well—an older couple arm in arm, and kids giggling as they ran ahead of their parents—but none paid attention to them.

"Thank you for coming to dinner with me tonight."

"Well, we had business to discuss."

"You know tonight was not about business," he said.

Yes, she did.

Angela extended her hand for the bottle, and he gave it to her. She took a swig, a little turned on that his mouth had touched the same spot only seconds ago.

"What happened to make you so afraid?" he asked gently.

She shivered though it wasn't cold. "I dated someone in the public eye before. It was messy and dramatic. Rumors, half-truths, and flat-out lies were told about us, especially me. The publicity strained our relationship, and we fought about things we shouldn't have fought about." She took another swig of the wine.

"The musician?" Andres said.

She shot a glance at him. "How did you…?"

"I have to be careful about the people I associate with."

"So I've been thoroughly investigated?"

"Yes."

"Wonderful," she said, though she wasn't surprised.

She'd only been twenty years old when it happened. Because of her father's work, she knew a lot of people in the music industry and hung out at one of the studios from time to time. That's how she met Liam, a well-known pop artist in his early twenties. When they started dating, Liam had been divorced from his wife for several months, though the news had been kept hush-hush to maintain the image of a sexy crooner who adored his wife, whom many thought was the inspiration for his love songs. He was charming and funny and she could admit now to being a little star struck.

When news broke about their relationship, her life turned upside down. His ex-wife had been with him since before he became a household name, his high school sweetheart, and although Angela had nothing to do with the breakup of their marriage, she was still deemed a homewrecker. She became persona non grata, and the fact that the singer and his ex-wife had a child together made the situation worse.

"Haven't you investigated me?" Andres asked.

"Only as much as Google allowed. You probably know more about me than I do myself." She grimaced.

"That, I doubt."

She glanced back at his security team.

"Do you ever get tired of it? Never being alone? The lack of privacy?"

"Lack of privacy? I haven't noticed," Andres quipped. He took the bottle from her.

"I'm not kidding."

Perhaps seeing the serious expression on her face swiped the amusement from his. "At times it's hard, yes. But I also live a life of luxury. You and I can spend time together without anyone knowing. No cameras, no articles about our private life. We could be like we were in Zamibia. Free to walk about together."

Angela hugged her torso, palms cupping her elbows. She

wanted to reach for more with him but hesitated because of her past experience.

"What exactly does a prince do?" she asked.

"That depends on the country, but in my case, over the past couple of years, I've taken over more and more of my grandfather's duties. Mostly ceremonial tasks such as welcoming dignitaries, attending state dinners and funerals, and traveling to other countries to establish or reconfirm diplomatic ties. Aside from that, the companies I and my advisors oversee for The Crown generate income for the royal family in excess of the taxes and tourism dollars we collect."

"Do your responsibilities ever overwhelm you?" Angela asked.

He paused for a moment. "No. My life could be more difficult. For example, as the reigning sovereign of Estoria, my grandfather Prince Felipe plays an important role in day-to-day politics. He is our official head of state and holds legislative, executive, and judicial power. His responsibilities are many, so you can imagine why as he gets older, the need to delegate becomes more important."

Andres stuck the bottle in the sand and walked over to her. "The chaos and publicity is my life. It doesn't have to be yours. We can meet in secret. Look at where we are." He spread his arms to encompass the area. "No one is paying attention to us. We had dinner and are walking on the beach. No cameras. No fans. Just you and me. It can be done. Trust me."

He took her hand and gently pulled her to him. His nose brushed her ear. "I can't explain it, but you're a part of me already. I missed you, and I know you missed me, too."

He was right. The gravitational pull to him was strong. She felt him underneath her skin, as if he were a part of her.

She looked into Andres's eyes. "Liam never defended me. He allowed people to say horrible things about me, about us, and he remained silent. I tried to understand. You can't respond to every rumor in the press, but some of them were so vile. And not once did he defend me."

That had been the most painful part—Liam's silence. His

silence had broken her heart, hurting more than the barbs printed in the paper. He even seemed to revel in the additional publicity, and there were times she wondered if he had fed false narratives to the press. His lips said he loved her, but his actions showed she was dispensable.

"I don't want to regret getting involved with you," Angela said in a low voice.

"You won't." He kissed the corner of her mouth.

"This is impossible."

"No, it's very possible." She heard the smile in his voice.

His arms slipped around her back and pulled her flush against his body.

She smoothed her palms over his hard chest. "I feel like I'm two minutes away from losing control when I'm with you."

"I know that feeling very well."

He kissed the side of her neck, and she dropped her head against his chest. Her fingers curled into the front of his shirt as her body heated to life.

"From the moment I saw you, I knew I needed to be with you, that you would change my life. I don't know how I knew, except that I've never felt this way before, even when I thought I was in love. There is no rush, Angela. We can take it slow. Say yes."

His words rustled over her skin like delicate cloth, and she turned her face toward his so their lips were only an inch apart.

She caressed his smooth, hard jaw. With a smile, she whispered, "I'll think about it. That's not a yes."

He smiled back. "But it's not a no."

"No, it's not a no."

10

"We're here," Andres said.

Angela lifted her head from the comfortable spot on his shoulder. She'd dozed off but had still been cognizant of what was happening around her. She vaguely remembered Andres talking on the phone, and recalled another time when the flight attendant entered to deliver refreshments.

She blinked, trying to get oriented to her surroundings. It seemed as if they'd gotten on the plane only minutes ago, and they were already back in Atlanta.

They were escorted into the same car with tinted windows that dropped them off earlier. Angela edged closer to Andres as they pulled away. He placed an arm around her and she reclaimed her comfy position against his shoulder.

One arm snaked around his torso. He hadn't left yet and she already missed him.

"How many more days will you be here before you have to go back?" she asked.

Andres's hand rubbed soothingly up and down her arm. "I leave tomorrow."

Her head popped up. She must have misunderstood. "Tomorrow? I-I assumed you would be here longer." He'd never given her an itinerary, but she thought he wanted to spend more time with her. Pain pinched beneath her breastbone at the thought of having to say goodbye.

"I would love to stay longer, but I can't. One of my roles is as ambassador of my country, and I'll spend the next ten days in Colombia, Argentina, and Uruguay. We're trying to establish stronger ties with South America, and I will be meeting with their heads of state and discussing opportunities for trade as well as tourism."

When he'd told Edgar about the trip to South America, she didn't realize it was so soon.

"When will you be back here, in the States?" she asked, desperation overwhelming her.

"Not for a month at least." The sadness in his eyes echoed in her chest.

"*A month*?" Four weeks sounded like four years, and four years sounded like an eternity. "What about the consulting project?"

"I'll give you the name of my COO, who you can work with on executing the plans."

Disappointment filled her heart to the brim, and she sat up all the way. "You came here with your grand gestures to impress me and talk about wanting to be with me, but a whole month will pass before I see you again? That's why this can't work." She scooted away from him and crossed her arms over her chest.

"What would you have me do? I have responsibilities, Angela. I can't cast them aside so simply."

"You're playing games, Andres." She glared at him.

"No, Angela, you're playing games. I have put all of my cards on the table. I want to be with you. Spend time with you. Make love to you. You're the one playing hard to get." His blue eyes flashed with annoyance.

"I am *not* playing hard to get. You're dismissing my reservations, as if they don't matter."

"I have addressed your reservations. We spent an entire night together without a single person approaching us. It *can* be done. I have a private island where we can vacation. I have homes or access to homes through friends and family that will allow us to meet up in almost any country in the world, without disturbance. You just have to get past your concerns about losing your privacy."

"You think those are my only concerns? How do I even know I can trust you? You're here now, with me, but who will you be with in South America? Will you see the Argentine pop star Martina Esposito when you're in her country? You were with her in Thailand not too long ago. I saw the pictures online. When you return to Europe, what then? You're so good at keeping your business private, you could have five other girlfriends for all I know. You want me to fall for your sweet words and wait around for months at a time while you're off doing God knows what? Ha." She gave another short laugh.

"Is that what you think? There are no other women, and if there were, I would have dropped them all for you. You mean that much to me. Haven't I proven that already, by coming here and showing you my willingness to carry on this relationship according to your terms? You don't believe what I say, that's fine. But what do my actions tell you? My actions, the way I treat you— will always show you how I feel, much better than any words can. Don't listen to what I say, look at what I do." He sat back and gazed out the window, one hand clenched on his thigh.

In an emotional state, she turned away from him. Her own fingers clenched on the seat beside her, nails digging into her palm. She sat in silent misery for several minutes, staring out at the night. They whizzed by other cars on the way to her house—a place she always thought of as a hideaway, an escape in a world filled with strife and obligations. Now, she likened it to a prison, where she'd be cordoned off until the next time she saw Andres. *If* she saw him again, considering the tense words they just spoke to each other.

A warm hand covered hers, and she turned to look at him. He eased her fingers open and held onto her hand.

"Come here," he said. He tugged gently, and her resolved melted.

She went to him and he folded her in his arms. They rode the rest of the way like that, her head against his chest, listening to the steady beat of his heart.

～

GUSTAVE OPENED the door at the curb in front of Angela's home. She and Andres exited onto the quiet street and walked slowly, hand in hand to the front door. The light came on and cast a yellow haze over their slow-moving bodies.

They stopped underneath the overhang and faced each other.

"I miss you already," Angela said. She gave a shaky laugh.

"Time will fly by. If I can come back sooner, I will."

She shook her head to dispel his need to make promises he might not be able to keep. "I'll be here, whenever you get back."

She opened the door but paused before going in. She turned around and, standing on her toes, gave him a small kiss on the lips. For a split second, he didn't move. Then with surprising speed, his arms clamped around her and dragged her against his body. He captured her mouth in a hungry kiss and plucked her lower lip between his right before he withdrew.

But she couldn't let go. She grasped his lapels and kept him close, pushing her tongue into a meeting with his.

His body was a distraction. His mouth an addiction. He was the greatest temptation she'd ever encountered. She didn't want the night to end.

Andres groaned.

"Stay," she whispered against his mouth.

"I can't… I should go back to my hotel. I have to leave early in the morning."

She ran her hands up his muscled torso and rubbed her thumbs over his nipples.

"Angela, what are you doing?" he asked in a hoarse voice. He sounded like a man at the end of his rope.

"I want you to stay, Andres. Not to sleep next to me like you did in Africa, but to make love to me before you leave. Give me something to hold onto until you come back."

The distance and time apart would only inflame the fire between them.

"As much as I want you, I don't want to rush this."

"It's no rush, I promise."

He laughed, his expression pained. "I want you to know that my feelings are pure. My intentions are—"

"Yes, yes, I believe you. All of that." She needed relief. She needed him now.

"Angela—"

"Andres," she said in a stern voice. She stepped into the house and stared at him. "If you don't get in here right now, don't bother. Ever."

Seconds ticked by at a snail's pace, and she wondered if she'd turned him off. Some men didn't like assertive women, but she'd never been shy about her need for sex or her enjoyment of the act.

Lucky for her, Andres smiled. Sexy, cocky, and with a grin as devilish as sin. "Your wish is my command."

He marched in and kicked the door shut. She reached for him, but he spun her around to face the wall and cupped her breasts from behind. Her desire flared to life, like dousing embers with gasoline. As he tweaked her engorged nipples, her knees buckled and she spread her palms against the wall to keep from crumbling into a heap at his feet.

He brushed away her hair and kissed her ear and jaw. "I have wanted to do this all night," he whispered huskily. "There are not enough hours in the day for everything I want to do to you."

She was acutely aware of him, his teeth at her neck, his long-fingered hands roaming her body.

"Do you see how much I want you?" he asked, grasping her

hips and pulling her back into his hardness. "I have been like this *all fucking night* because of you."

His angry confession made her hornier. She twisted around and kissed him hard, lifting her leg and angling her hips to rub her swollen sex against the stiffness in his pants. Her panties were damp. Her nipples were hard. This need for him, this unprecedented arousal, had been building to this point since the first night they met. She shoved her fingers into his thick hair and tilted her head to get at his mouth.

He cradled her bottom and lifted her from the floor, and then she wrapped her legs around his waist. When her back hit the wall, his hips plowed into hers. He sprinkled kisses onto her neck and she arched her throat into the heady sensation of his soft lips. She ached for closer contact and moved against him as the pulse between her legs begged for release.

"What about your guards and the driver? Should we send them away?" Angela panted.

"They'll wait. They cannot leave me."

They kissed again. Hungry. Chaotic. With a clash of tongues and moist lips that was erotic and wonderfully messy.

Andres tore his mouth from hers. "Where is your bedroom?"

"Upstairs."

He made haste, climbing the steep stairs with her wrapped around him.

11

"Don't move. Let me taste you," Andres whispered against her mouth.

His drugging kisses were simply divine and made her limbs feel languid, as if she could melt into the floor. She breathed him in, anxious to have more, and the wine they drank on the beach teased her taste buds as his tongue danced with hers. He brushed her lips with that same wicked tongue and grasped a handful of hair to tilt back her head.

"I could stay on your mouth all night, but there's so much more of you that I want to enjoy."

He nibbled on her neck and sensitive collarbone, the whole time whispering words of Spanish in a husky undertone. With bites and licks, he sampled her skin, leaving her damn near incoherent in the wake of his touch. Little by little, he took control of her will and kept her immobile so he could have his fill.

He tugged her blouse out of her pants, pulled it over her head, and tossed it aside. Then his gaze dropped to her lace-covered breasts.

"Stay right there," he whispered, and she couldn't move. She only wanted to do whatever he commanded.

He stepped behind her and unclipped the front clasp of the bra and freed her breasts into his hands.

Angela leaned back into him and sighed with pleasure as his fingers skated over the soft mounds and then kneaded their fullness. His thumbs rubbed her nipples until they became achingly hard, full and taut under the ministrations of his hands.

She felt as if she had wanted this man forever and shivered as he swept her hair to one side and kissed the unveiled nape of her neck. His fingers slid down to her pants and he released the button and then lowered the zipper.

His warm hand snaked beneath the waistband of her panties and cupped her sex. Her belly clenched and pressure built in her loins from the gentle touch. The pleasure he gave was so intense that her breath tangled in her chest, unable to break free. She had to remind herself to breathe and how to stand upright because her knees threatened to buckle underneath her.

"*Mi amor*...you're so wet."

His fingers spread the folds apart and used the slickness to massage her clit in deliberately slow circles. Her breathing turned ragged and she covered his hand with hers. She didn't want him to stop, but the torturous movements were almost too much to handle.

Andres's next move was to push her pants down her legs. He helped her out of them and her shoes and then he turned her to face him. His eyes darkened as he looked at her, standing without a stitch of clothing on her body.

"I knew you'd be beautiful, but..." he said huskily. He lapsed into Spanish, whispering words she didn't understand, but the adoration in his eyes were as clear as a neon sign.

They moved to the bed and she lay down, watching with anticipation as he performed a brief striptease, unveiling his body with slow movements, first his shirt, then his pants and underwear. Finally, he was as naked as she was, and she could admire him in all his glory.

His tight body was a thing of beauty, crafted from regular exercise and playing sports. His abs were nothing but a hard six-pack, and his legs and thighs, sprinkled with dark hair, were thick and muscular. Her eyes zeroed in on his hard length and she couldn't help but think that it was extremely unfair for one man to be so well-endowed.

Andres bent over her supine body and kissed her with a hungry, mind-numbing kiss. She moaned as their fused mouths dipped and sucked at each other. Then he lowered his head to feast on her breasts while his hands smoothed over her waist and the fullness of her hips. Every line and curve in her body was explored by him. From shoulder to ankle, he grew familiar with her, kneading and caressing and touching and squeezing until she was a trembling, writhing, mess of a woman begging for her lover to put an end to her misery.

She speared her fingers into his hair and arched her hips toward him, grinding her pelvis against his hard length, signaling a readiness to receive him whenever he was ready to take her. But he took his time. His tip teased her opening, sliding between her wet lips but refusing to enter as if he wanted to make sure that she knew he was in charge.

He went back to her breasts and suckled each peak, teasing with his tongue and torturing with his teeth. The entire time, a hand between her legs stroked with lazy indulgence, as if he had all the time in the world. It was almost too much to bear.

He was trying to kill her. He was trying to make her lose her mind, and that's exactly what would happen if he didn't take her soon.

Her hand reached lower and covered his veined length. She shifted beneath him until he was centered at her core. He stopped moving, and she squeezed and felt him pulsate in her hand.

"Andres, please. Take me now. *Now.*"

With a deft motion, he forced her onto her belly. His hands stroked down her spine and smoothed past her waist to her bottom, where he squeezed her fleshy butt cheeks. Angela arched her back and held her breath, enthralled by his electrifying touch and the anticipation of what he would do to her next.

Andres lifted her to her knees and bore down on her back, sliding deep between her sprawled thighs with an aggressiveness that made her gasp and grab a handful of the sheets. Her head fell forward and her hair tumbled around her face. The wanting and aching was finally over. Now only fullness and satisfaction reigned.

The next hard thrust forced her face into the pillow. Andres placed a firm hand at her neck to keep her in that position, and she willingly succumbed to the force of his will. With a relentless rhythm, he pounded into her with increasing intensity. Her limbs trembled as she urged him deeper, angling her hips higher and clenching her muscles around him.

"Yes, yes..." she moaned into the pillow. Eyes shut tight, she concentrated on the erotic sensation of him driving behind her and how each measured stroked slapped his hips against her ass.

"Do you feel that? Do you feel how good we are together?"

"Yes," she replied, her answer ending on a tortured wail.

She was so close. She wanted to prolong the torment but needed to get release. Both sides warred within her.

Without warning, Andres pulled out, and she let loose an angry growl as her orgasm was snatched away so suddenly.

She rolled over onto her back and looked up at him. Grasping her thighs, he shoved back into her, and her face crumbled at the exquisite pleasure of having him fill her again.

"I want to watch you come," he said.

He seemed to abandon all control as he fucked her hard and fast. With each thrust he brought her closer to climax, and Angela dug her heels into the mattress. The reason she kept up with his manic pace was because of the adrenaline coursing through her veins. Up and down went the motion of their bodies. Up and down went the mattress at her back.

"Look at me. *Mírame*," he demanded.

Their eyes met, and he slammed into her harder. She yielded to his strength and his relentless pace.

His blue eyes flashed down at her and a lock of hair fell across his brow. "I want all of you. *Dame todo, mi amor,*" he whispered, stretching her arms above her head. He held her in position and lowered his lips to her neck. "*Todo.*"

Her head arched back and her mouth fell open, eyes staring out at the night through the skylight. He added a circular rhythm to the motion of his hips, and that was her downfall.

An orgasm burst from her loins and she cried out. Her mind spun out of control, her feverish body pulsing and shaking around him. As she came undone, completely unraveled, his own body became stiff and he dropped his head to her shoulder. His fingers tightened around her wrists and he let loose a throaty groan, pushing and pushing, harder and harder until there was nothing left to give.

"Andres, she breathed in a shaky voice.

"I'm here."

He released her arms and she closed them around his neck.

"Andres," she whispered again, panting. She pressed her face into the side of his neck and held on tight as aftershocks rippled through both of their bodies.

ANDRES DRESSED SLOWLY, aware of Angela's eyes on him as he slipped into the clothes he'd so readily removed last night. Residual lust hummed in his veins, but he couldn't spend any more time here without cutting it close. Daybreak was coming, and he had a flight to catch. He'd have less time to prep for his meetings and would have to sleep on the plane. Not that he was complaining. He'd enjoyed every single minute with Angela.

He finished dressing and sat on the edge of the mattress. She lay on her side under the rumpled covers. She was a vision of loveliness, with her pink lips swollen from his kisses and her golden skin illuminated by the moonlight filtering through the open skylight.

With a heavy heart, he stroked his fingers through her soft hair, brushing back tendrils so he could get a good look at her face. He saw the disappointment in her eyes, but he had to go.

"I'll call you soon."

"Okay."

He dropped a kiss on the corner of her mouth and stood before he changed his mind and abandoned his trip to South America.

He walked across the room.

"Goodbye, Andres," she said.

He turned to look at her one more time. "*Hasta luego*, Angela," he replied.

Then he was gone.

12

Seated in a cream leather chair in the royal plane, Andres watched with relief as Sweden disappeared from view.

"Your Highness." The blonde flight attendant's soft voice caught his attention as with a sympathetic smile she set a vodka on the rocks on the table in front of him.

"Thank you," he said gratefully. She disappeared as quietly as she came.

Since he'd managed to halt the building of the new casino-hotel on Estorian soil, Andres had become obsessed with the idea of transforming the nation into a leader in green living. His visit to Sweden had solely been to glean knowledge about their progress in environmental issues. The Scandinavian country made investing in green technology a priority and believed in conserving resources for future generations. Their ideology impressed him. While he had gained some valuable information from talking to the Swedish EPA about their policies, his visit with the royal family had been nerve-racking.

Once again, the Swedish king's distant cousin was present, and she made no secret that she would like Andres to consider her a candidate for his future spouse. She was a lovely woman with whom he'd had a fling two summers ago, but since then he'd always done his utmost best not to lead her on, making it clear that he had no interest in getting married.

Not after seeing how miserable his grandfather and father were in their marriages. They'd sacrificed for the country, marrying noblewomen they didn't love simply because it was tradition, because it was expected. He saw the misery between his parents, and it was an open secret that his grandfather used to have a mistress with whom he had been in love, but Felipe's own father had not given him permission to marry her because he hadn't deemed her worthy.

Since Andres expected Juan to be the successor to the throne because of his age and work with Felipe, that made his anti-marriage stance even easier. He had no requirements to produce an heir. Besides, he simply wasn't interested in her anymore, particularly now. He was only interested in one woman.

Angela. He couldn't erase the memory of her or the taste of her lips. With one look, one touch, she set fire to his blood.

A month after his trip to South America, he'd flown back to Atlanta and she spent the weekend with him at the Winthrop Hotel. The hotel chain had several locations in the metro Atlanta area, but that location was their most exclusive, known for maintaining the privacy of its high-profile guests. He rented out two floors for the entire year to make it easy for him to come and go as he pleased, and to ensure his privacy and house the staff traveling with him.

Wearing a baseball cap low on his brow, he and Angela once went to a movie and sat in the back, with his guards flanking them at either end of the row. The next day he picked her up after an official event. He'd craved an American cheeseburger, and they went through the drive-thru in the limo. She'd had a fit giggling behind the tinted windows of the backseat as the cashier stared curiously at Gustave ordering them bacon cheeseburgers, fries, and milkshakes.

That was only two weeks ago, and it felt like an eternity.

Deep in thought, he sipped from his glass. Why should he wait to see her when he could arrange to be back in the States, under the guise of checking on the firm or coming up with some diplomatic reason? Why not see her now?

Impulsively, he flipped open a panel on the table in front of him and pressed a button.

"Yes, Your Highness," the flight attendant answered.

"Bring me a secure line."

Less than a minute later, she reentered the space and handed him a satellite phone. He dialed Angela's direct number at work, and she answered on the second ring.

"Hello, Andres."

His belly warmed at the sound of her voice, and he rested his elbow on the chair rest, a smile spreading across his face. "Hello. I was thinking about you and wondered what you were doing on this fine Friday."

"It's morning here, so I'm working. And you?"

"I just left a meeting in Sweden."

"Was it to discuss the environmental policies you want to implement?"

Andres relaxed into the chair and welcomed the conversation. Managing an intercontinental relationship was difficult, to say the least, but they spoke often, usually after she left work, which meant late nights or very early morning phone calls for him because of the five-hour time difference. Not that he minded. He liked talking to her.

They both enjoyed outdoor activities like hiking, jogging, horseback riding, and she listened, really listened, when he talked. Her take on ideas were refreshing, and she wasn't afraid to disagree with him and challenged his ideas on various topics, from anything as complex as world politics to as simple as his taste in music.

"Yes, their environmental policies are advanced to our own, and I plan to do some follow-up at a later date, once I've had a chance to talk to our commission. But the reason I called is because I want to see you, not next weekend or the one after that or the next. This weekend. I can send a plane for you and you could meet me on Isla de Vasquez. I haven't built an airstrip yet, so you'll have to land in Puerto Rico and take a helicopter to the island."

His grandfather had purchased the private island from a software billionaire. It included an over-ten-thousand-square-foot open-air mansion set on a small hill with panoramic views worthy of a postcard. The house overlooked a pristine beach and aqua-blue water, along with smaller villas that could be rented out to guests. He didn't get to visit often, but over sixty staff members maintained the properties year-round, which allowed him to pop in at a moment's notice.

Angela groaned. "That's a tempting offer, but I can't. I'm swamped with work."

"Even on the weekend? You can't take a couple of days off?"

She sighed, and he waited impatiently for her answer.

"I want to see you, I do, but…"

"But what?" Initially he thought his schedule would be the problem, but her damn job was a thorn in his side. Everything they did—from talking on the phone to how much time they could spend in each other's company, was dictated by Myers-Gomez. "You can arrive tonight, so you don't have to miss work, and spend the next two days work-free on a private island in the Caribbean. We could go horseback riding, walk on the beach, or simply relax seaside. Isn't that tempting?"

"I could use the break," she said quietly.

The knot in his stomach loosened. "Let me give you a break."

She laughed. "You're so convincing. Fine! You talked me into it. If I'm going to be gone all weekend and really take a break, I need to get as much done as I can today. Then I'll knock off around six-ish, get home, and be packed within an hour."

"I'll have a car at your door by seven. And I'll see you tonight."

"Yes, tonight," she said softly.

They spoke for a few more minutes, then Andres hung up and called up front to the pilot. "Change of plans. Set a new course for Isla de Vasquez."

THIS PLACE WAS PARADISE. Angela stood on the landing, leaning against the wooden railing that overlooked the beach. She wore a gauzy white cover-up over her black bikini and kept her hair loose, letting the cool breeze coming off the water blow the strands around her face. This was just what she needed. Time away to just…breathe.

Last night when she touched down on the helipad, Andres met her right away and swept her into his arms as if they hadn't seen each other in months instead of only weeks. Her heart thrilled at his enthusiastic greeting, and she wondered, not for the first time, just where this relationship was headed.

The man was a prince, for God's sake, and she held no illusions about princes riding up on white horses to sweep you away to a charmed life. Yet spending time with him gave her a glimpse into what she'd been missing in other relationships, particularly the one with Liam. He'd courted the spotlight, needing to see and be seen to further his career. That wasn't the case with Andres. While there was some notoriety because of who he was, he didn't care about impressing anyone. He didn't need to. That made spending time with him all the more enjoyable. She could unwind and cast off the stress of her career when she was with him.

She swept her fingers through her hair and watched as Andres came jogging up the beach, bare-chested from his morning run.

He panted as he rushed up the stairs, fit body glistening, and his dark, windswept hair damp with sweat around the edges.

She handed him a bottle of cold water, which he gratefully accepted. He took a huge swallow.

"You should have joined me," he said.

"I wanted to relax. Isn't that what you promised me, rest and relaxation?"

"You remember what I said?"

"I remember everything you say, Your Highness." She bit her bottom lip and watched his eyes darken with lust.

"You know I love it when you say that," he said in a low voice.

He set down the bottle, and Angela squealed as he tugged her closer with an arm around her waist and dipped her over his arm with an indulgent kiss. Her arms fastened around his neck, and she kissed him back with fervor and passion.

When they straightened, she was breathless and her heart raced excitedly.

Andres kept his forehead pressed to hers. "Have you eaten breakfast yet?" he asked softly.

"No, I was waiting for you," she whispered.

"I am hungry, but not for food," he said.

"I'm hungry, too. But not for food," she admitted.

Due to her late arrival last night, they hadn't made love. They'd simply curled up next to each other and slept through the night, until she was awakened by him moving around early this morning right before he went for a jog. She'd intended to take a morning dip in the infinity pool but set aside the idea to wait for his return.

"I need a shower, and then I'll show you how much I missed you."

He swooped her up in his arms and marched toward the bedroom, past the chef and mixologist who tended the open bar.

"We're going to be busy for a while. Do not disturb," he called out to them. Both men smiled knowingly.

Angela's cheeks heated. "You're awful," she said, burying her face in his neck.

He only chuckled, and carried her like a conqueror claiming his prize, through the house to his private quarters where he shut the door on the outside world and showed just how much he'd missed her.

13

A ngela blinked as she slowly woke up. She heard Andres in the bathroom.

After they made love in the morning, they spent a busy day swimming and then horseback riding over some of the rougher terrain of the island. Afterward, they returned for a late lunch and fell into bed and made love for a second time.

The bedroom had been decorated in such a way as to incorporate the natural environment into the interior. Dark woods, some of which had been chosen from the surrounding area, were used to create the furniture, and white curtains billowed in the breeze coming in through the open windows. She stretched in the wide king bed, covered with soft white sheets that made her not want to get up.

Andres had opened the doors that took up a large portion of one wall and led onto the landing. That allowed a brisk breeze to sweep through the doors and out the open windows in the back, so there was no need for air conditioning.

She slipped from the bed and donned a loose-fitting maxi dress with three-quarter-length sleeves and a hemline that swirled around her ankles as she walked onto the landing. The table was set with covered dishes, and she peeked under one of the domes and found a bowl of fresh fruit—sliced mangoes, oranges, and strawberries. She picked up a piece of mango and slid it into her mouth, moaning as the sweet flavor doused her tongue.

Andres came up behind her and nuzzled her neck. He smelled fresh from another shower. "I'm so glad you came."

"Me, too," she whispered.

"Has any man kissed you since I've seen you last?"

"No."

"So you're mine and mine alone?"

"Maybe..." she said.

"Maybe?" he repeated, sounding affronted. "Not good enough."

"Are *you* mine?" Angela asked, casting a look over her shoulder.

"You still have doubts?"

"Just wondering how long this will last."

"As long as you allow it." He set a black square box on the wooden railing in front of her.

"What's this?"

"Open it."

She didn't hesitate. Inside was an exquisite piece of fine jewelry —a diamond halo bangle that sparkled in the natural light. It must've cost a small fortune.

"You like it?" Andres asked, snapping the jewelry onto her wrist. "I love it."

"You don't think it's too much? Or I shouldn't have bought it?"

He watched her oddly, and she wondered if she should have said one of those things. But she loved it and didn't see the point in pretending that she didn't.

"No. It's extravagant, but who wouldn't be grateful to receive a gift like this?"

His face transformed into a smile. "You are really something, you know that? I can't tell you how often I've given a gift and been made to feel almost guilty about it. Some women act as if they don't deserve nice things, which makes it hard to know what to give them. Or even if to give them anything at all."

"I'm not one of those women. I enjoy gifts—giving as well as receiving. Feel free to surprise me anytime you like."

They both laughed.

"Good," he said.

She sobered and stroked his jaw with her fingertips. Standing closer, she whispered, "In all seriousness, thank you."

"My pleasure." He dropped a kiss to her lips. "Your honesty is refreshing."

"Yes, honesty is important, isn't it?"

"Yes."

"Being honest goes both ways, Andres."

He frowned. "I've always been honest with you, since the beginning."

"Except for when you didn't tell me you were a prince."

"Ancient history," he said.

She stroked his bare arm, smoothing her palm over the hair-sprinkled skin. "You're keeping secrets, about other things, too. About your family."

His demeanor changed as all humor drained from him. "I've told you all you need to know," he said irritably. He faced the sea and rested his forearms on the railing.

"You like honesty and want me to be an open book, and I expect the same from you."

"I haven't kept anything from you. I am an open book. Ask me anything."

"I can ask you anything. Really?"

"Anything but state secrets," he said, with a small attempt at humor. His lips turned up minutely at the corners, but his blue eyes remained troubled, the way someone looked when they were awaiting bad news.

Angela brushed her thumbnail along the scar on his left brow.

"Tell me the story about this. Because you didn't just fall down the stairs."

"Angela…"

"Why can't you talk to me and be honest? Is it really that bad that you can't share whatever happened to you with me?"

He sighed. "You're a difficult woman."

"And you're a difficult man. We're perfect for each other."

He looked at her from the corner of his eye and still didn't respond. She decided to wait him out. Finally, he sighed again.

"I fell down the palace stairs."

"That's not all."

He glanced at her.

"Please." Whatever happened to cause that scar was important, and if he trusted her with this piece of information, sharing that secret part of himself could add a new dimension to their relationship.

He swallowed. "You're right, I did not just fall down the stairs. I had some help." The next words seemed difficult for him, but he finally said in a low voice, "From my father."

Angela gasped. The secret was worse than she imagined. She could only see Andres's profile, but pain was evident in the tautness of his cheekbones.

"I'm sorry, if you don't want to talk about what happened, you don't have to."

"I want to." He bowed his head and gathered himself. A rueful smile turned up the corners of his mouth. "My father is a raging alcoholic. My grandfather did everything he could to…fix him, I suppose you could say Counseling, acupuncture, therapists, and hypnosis at one time, from what I understand. My father did not change. He was belligerent and verbally abusive to my mother, the palace staff, and anyone who came around him when he was intoxicated. They called those times his rages. His periods of drunkenness became more frequent as I grew older, and my grandfather kept him from most of his official duties because of it. Grandfather took on those tasks himself or assigned them to others."

He swallowed again, and pain reentered his face in the form of a grimace. "I'll never forget that day, the weekend of my birthday. My grandfather had planned a small party—nothing too extravagant—by our standards, anyway. A magician performed tricks for me and my friends, and later a group of us went horseback riding. We did anything that I wanted to do. I went the whole day without seeing him, but I wanted to. I was disappointed but had a good time with friends and family. His rejection on my birthday consumed me. I don't know why, but I wanted to see him."

"He's your father. It's understandable that you wanted to spend time with him despite his behavior," Angela said quietly.

He nodded. "Anyway, he and my mother had been sleeping apart for some time, so I went to his room to look for him. I didn't want anything—nothing material, anyway. Maybe a hug. A simple 'happy birthday, son' would have made my year.

"He wasn't in his room, so I left, but he caught me exiting. He'd been drinking recently because I smelled the liquor on him. He demanded to know what I was doing in his room. I told him nothing, but he flew into a rage. You see, he had told me many times not to touch his things. I hadn't touched anything in his room, but he didn't believe me. He started yelling at me and accused me of being a thief. He said that I was a perfect little shit who stole his happiness from the day I was born."

Angela covered his hand with one of hers. His secret was so much worse than she imagined, and now she regretted pushing him to share.

"He chased me down the hall. I ran as fast as I could, but he caught me at the stairs and grabbed me by the neck of my shirt. 'Stay out of my things!' he said. And then he…he hit me, with the back of his hand, and I fell down the marble staircase."

Angela wrapped her arms around his torso and lifted her gaze to his. "I'm sorry. I can't imagine how you must have felt."

His jawline went rigid. "I was knocked unconscious by the fall and woke up in bed with my grandfather over me and a bandage covering my head. I had bruised ribs and a broken wrist from where I'd apparently tried to break my fall."

"So that's why your father is no longer in Estoria?" Angela asked.

Andres nodded. "My grandfather sent him away the next day. He's been exiled to Spain ever since then, under constant surveillance by a handler and a security team. They keep him safe and out of trouble."

"That happened when you were eight. Have you had any contact with him since?"

"Very little. We've spoken on the phone, and I visited him a handful of times. Strong drink and a rough life have aged him. He looked nothing like the man I once adored."

"What happened to your mother?"

"She left soon after my grandfather approved her divorce from my father."

"Approved?"

He nodded. "All royal marriages and divorces must be approved by the reigning monarch. She was allowed to divorce my father and leave the country on one condition—that she leave me in Estoria to be raised by my grandfather. She left and we've barely spoken since."

Angela's heart broke for him. She rested her temple against his shoulder.

"My father was unhappy for a long time. He hated his role as prince and turned to drinking to deal with the stress of his position, the stress of having to provide an heir and marry someone whom he probably didn't love. He transferred that bitterness onto me, and eventually it turned to hate."

Angela glanced up at his profile. "You were a *child*. You were *eight*."

"None of that matters. Hate is not rational. It's toxic and erodes common sense and destroys relationships."

Angela nodded her agreement. "I know what you mean."

He looked at her questioningly.

"My sister is like your father. She's fourteen years older than me, and when I was little I idolized her, but she couldn't stand me."

She explained that Martin married Tessa years after his divorce from Rebecca's mother, but Rebecca still blamed Tessa for taking away her father. She told him how she wished she'd been able to have a good relationship with her sister and envied other people when she saw how close they were to their siblings. She wanted the same type of relationship.

"Now it's my turn to be sorry," Andres said. He lifted her hand and kissed the back of it. "I'm sorry you had to go through that."

"I'm sorry *you* had to go through that."

"I've never told anyone that story."

"Thank you for sharing it with me. I promise I won't repeat it. You can trust me, Andres."

"I know. And you can trust me," he said.

"We didn't completely lose out. I have my parents and good friends. You have your grandfather and good friends. Our lives could be worse."

"Yes, they could be. And right now, our lives are getting better, don't you agree?" His voice lowered and he dropped his gaze to her mouth.

"Yes. Definitely better," she agreed.

When he bent his head to kiss her, she lifted her lips to meet him halfway.

ON SUNDAY, Angela lay on top of Andres with her cheek against his back. His skin was so soft she didn't want to move.

The sound of the waves crashing outside saddened her. In a little while, she'd have to leave, and she didn't want to.

"I better go." She kissed his shoulder and rolled off him onto the mattress. She stared up at the ceiling. The weekend had been way too short. Where had the time gone?

"Stay with me."

"You know I can't."

"Of course you can. Quit your job and let me take care of you. Then you wouldn't have to worry about clients and schedules and getting back to work after a fun, relaxing weekend."

Was he joking or serious? She grinned, smoothing away a lock of hair that had fallen onto his forehead. "Be a kept woman, you mean? Sure."

She slipped from the bed and went over to the luggage.

"Is that such a crazy idea?"

Angela searched for clothes to change into after her shower. "Have you done it before?" She pulled a few articles of clothing from the suitcase.

"I have."

Angela straightened and looked at him. "Are you serious? You *paid* a woman to be with you?"

"I didn't pay her to be with me. I covered her expenses so she'd have more time to spend with me."

"However you choose to define the relationship, I'm not interested."

"Why not?" Andres sat up in the bed.

"Because I'm way too independent for that." She tossed him a saucy grin over her shoulder. "Care to join me in the shower?"

He jumped up from the bed, and she squealed, scampering into the bathroom ahead of him.

Later, he escorted her out to the helipad and the waiting helicopter, which would take her back to Puerto Rico for the flight home. They exchanged a lingering kiss, and then she climbed aboard. She watched him below, hands tucked into his trousers, face solemn as the wind from the rotating blades whipped his clothes and hair into a frenzy. When tears pricked the back of her eyelids, she turned away.

Leaving him was harder than she'd expected. She cursed her

maddening, out-of-control need for him. If she didn't need him so much, then leaving wouldn't be so hard.

Her fingers clenched in her lap. Would she always feel like this when they separated, or would the achiness become easier to bear over time? She hoped the latter. Because the wrench in her gut was already close to unbearable.

14

Wasim's wooden mallet connected with the ball, landing a hard blow that sent it in the opposite direction toward the goal of their opponents. The crowd went wild as a potential victory for the Diamond Team was now a possibility.

"¡*Vamos!*" Andres yelled.

He pulled on the horse's reins and completed an agile pivot, racing downfield after the ball. He galloped alongside a member of Los Caballeros, the opposition team from Argentina, and reached down and swung his mallet, narrowly avoiding a collision with the other man's horse.

The bell rang to let them know only thirty seconds remained in the match. The third member of the Diamond Team, a professional player from Estoria named Jorge, came in from the side and hit the ball toward Andres. He in turn sent it downfield to his friend Kofi.

Kofi raced toward it, seconds ahead of the opposing team member, and swung, performing an elegant shot under the horse's neck. With only seconds to spare, the ball swept through the Los Caballeros goalposts and the crowd jumped to their feet, clapping and yelling.

"Yes!" Andres yelled. He stood in the stirrups and threw up his hands at the victory.

Though it was only an exhibition game, this was an important win. He, Wasim, and Kofi were patrons of the Diamond Team. They'd poured millions into the team for training, travel, and horses. In exchange, they won the occasional tournament and got to play in them with the professionals. This win was one they'd remember for a long time to come. They'd beat a team of Argentinians.

Andres's horse trotted up beside Kofi's. "Good job."

Wasim and Jorge rode up alongside them.

"Well played," said Jorge.

The four men did a victory lap, waving their hands at the cheering spectators. After long moments of adulation, they shook hands with the four men from the other team and took photos with the trophy.

The three princes quickly changed into collared shirts and slacks and walked toward a white VIP private cabana located field side. A second match started soon and they wanted to be in position to watch the team they funded compete. Their progress was slow as they shook hands along the way and accepted congratulations from the men and women who intercepted their progress.

Kofi's cousin, Imani, greeted them with a smile as they approached. She was dressed like many of the other women, in a spectacular white hat and a yellow and white sundress that brightened her dark brown skin.

"Well, congratulations are in order," she said, standing from the round table. Attendants waited at another table filled with all sorts of alcoholic options and gourmet hors d'oeuvres.

"Was there ever any doubt?" Wasim said.

"Of course, but now you have a tournament trophy to add to your list of accomplishments." Her eyes focused on something in the distance. "Oh my goodness, is that Nacho Figueras?" Imani covered her mouth and her eyes widened.

They all turned and sure enough, the famous polo player stood near the field with his wife, in conversation with a man Andres didn't recognize.

"You realize we just won our match?" Wasim said.

Imani smiled sweetly. "Yes, but we all know that was a fluke. No offense, gentlemen. Nacho is a true champion, and he's very good looking. I have to meet him."

"You know he's married?" Wasim asked, sounding irritated.

"That doesn't mean I can't say hello, and you promised to introduce me, remember?" Imani grinned and batted her eyelashes at him.

Wasim groaned.

"You can't go back on your promise now."

Imani looped an arm through his, and Wasim grunted and muttered in Arabic.

"We'll be right back," Imani sang, dragging him away.

Andres chuckled and sat down at the table, stretching his legs out before him. "She's like a ball of fire," he remarked.

"Always," Kofi agreed. "If Wasim is not careful, he's going to get burned."

"What do you mean?"

Kofi joined him at the table. "I'm not a fool. I see the way he looks at my cousin."

Wasim had denied his interest to Andres, but their flirtations with each other indicated there was some interest on both their parts.

"And you're worried about Wasim and not her?"

"I've seen Imani break hearts before. Trust me, he has no idea what he's in for."

Andres chuckled. He had not expected Kofi to take this point of view. He'd fully expected him to be protective of Imani, but clearly she could hold her own. He now worried about his good friend, Wasim, too.

Andres pulled one of the other chairs closer and stretched his arm along the top. "How are things in Zambia? Settled, I hope."

They hadn't had a chance to talk before the match started. Kofi had experienced several tragedies since the wedding. One of their mines had collapsed because of foul play, causing death and injury that plagued his friend's conscience though there had been no way for him to know ahead of time of the sinister motives of the culprits. Then, as if that wasn't enough, a member of his staff had done the unthinkable by threatening the lives of members of the royal family.

"We're coping and doing much better. Justice was swift," Kofi said in a grave voice.

"And Dahlia, she's adjusting to her new life?"

"Yes. As you know, the transition hadn't been easy for her at first, but she's gotten a lot better." Kofi's mood changed, and he leaned forward with a grin. "I have some good news. I wanted to tell you and Wasim in person. Dahlia is pregnant."

"What? Congratulations! That's cause for a celebration."

He signaled to a waiter, and when he caught the man's eye, told him to bring over a bottle of champagne. He did so, as well as set a starter plate of hors d'oeuvres in front of them.

The two men shared a toast.

Andres held up his glass. "Congratulations! To new beginnings, marriage, changing diapers, and all the things I used to think I didn't want."

They touched their glasses together. Kofi took a sip from his and then set it on the table. "Did I understand you correctly? You *used* to think you didn't want? That's past tense."

"My stance on marriage has…evolved, you might say."

Kofi's eyebrows shot up. "When did this happen?"

"I met someone."

Kofi narrowed his eyes. "Are you Prince Andres of Estoria, confirmed bachelor, from the rogue principality of Estoria?"

"I assure you, it is I." Andres sipped from his glass, amused at his friend's teasing.

"This sounds serious. You're not joking at all, are you? Whoever this woman is, you really like her." Kofi popped an olive in his mouth.

"Yes." Andres ran a hand through his hair. "She consumes me. I wanted her to come today, but she couldn't get time off from work."

"Aha, so she's a working woman. How did you meet her?"

Andres looked steadily at his friend. "At your wedding."

"Oh really? What's her name?"

"Angela." He waited for Kofi to connect the dots.

"Angela…" Kofi stared at him. "Angela Lipscomb, Dahlia's best friend?"

"Yes."

"You've been seeing her since the wedding?" Kofi asked.

"Well, not too long after the wedding. She's different, to say the least. Beautiful. Funny. And is not afraid to challenge me."

"I sense a 'but' coming," Kofi said.

"*But* she's also independent and headstrong and won't do what I tell her."

"I know all about that," Kofi said, referring to his wife.

They both chuckled.

"It must be difficult with her living in the States and you living here in Europe."

"It's impossible." Andres sighed. "And her independence makes having a relationship harder. She loves her job and wants to keep it, but consulting keeps her busy. She's in Hong Kong at the moment."

"Hmmm, I understand how that could be a problem."

"Otherwise, she's perfect."

"Is there any flexibility in her career at all?" Kofi asked.

"Not that I can see or that she seems willing to take advantage of."

"How serious are you about her? Do you want her to give up her career so you can spend more time together? Are you talking marriage?"

"Marriage, I'm not sure," Andres admitted, though the thought came to him more often lately. "I tested the waters already, and she doesn't seem open to giving up her career." He wasn't even sure if she fully understood what he was asking back on Isla de Vasquez when he suggested that she quit her job.

He could see himself married to Angela, working together in the palace, riding horses around the island in their downtime. But was that something she would consider? Could she walk away from her family, her career, and country, to be with him?

"One of our biggest problems is that she doesn't want the publicity that comes with being with a man like me. One of her exes was in the music industry, and she wants no part of public life again."

"Well then, you have to respect that. But if you're not sure about marriage, and you simply want to be with her, does anyone have to know? No one knows now. No one knew about your grandfather's mistress, if I recall correctly what you told me."

"Officially, no one *knew* about her, but everyone knew," Andres said dryly.

"I see." Kofi swirled his glass on the table for a moment while his gaze swept the field. "If you're going to spend more time with Angela, one of you has to give, and we both know that will be her. How long ago did you broach the topic of giving up her career?"

"It's been a couple of weeks." Andres sipped champagne.

"Maybe it's time to bring it up again. Buy her a place in Estoria or in Spain so that she could be closer. And she doesn't have to give up working entirely. Employ her at one of your family's companies."

Andres liked that idea and it might appeal to Angela. She enjoyed working, and that way she wouldn't be bored. "I'll think about it."

He thought about his grandfather's arrangement and knew he could never live that life. Felipe had married a woman he didn't love and kept the woman he did love away from the public eye. They'd loved each other, but they'd both been miserable because they couldn't truly be together. And now his grandfather had no one to spend his twilight years with. His wife had died and his mistress had long ago moved on.

Over the loudspeaker, the announcer said the next match started in five minutes.

Andres tapped his fingers on the table top. He'd convinced Angela to enter into a relationship with him, despite the fact that he was a public figure. Surely he could take his negotiations skills even further and figure out how to convince her to move to Europe. Like Kofi suggested, she could keep working if she wanted to, but then they could be together more often.

He liked that idea and would start working on a plan right away.

15

U nder the soft duvet cover in the hotel suite, Angela nestled against the warmth of Andres's body. As always, last night they'd shared intense and erotic love-making that she would rewind in her mind until the next time he came to town.

Unfortunately, she had to get up now to start the day. She rolled away from his warmth with a groan.

"Where are you going?" Amusement colored his voice. He closed the distance between them and pressed his lips against the middle of her back where the sheet had fallen away.

His mouth sent shivers down her spine, and Angela shoved her thick hair from her face and rose onto her elbows.

"I have to go to work," she said.

"Not yet. I have something for you." He reached into the drawer of the bedside table and handed her a black velvet box with the name of a European jeweler printed in gold on top.

Angela sat up against the pillows and kept the linens tucked under her arms to cover her nakedness. "What is this?" She playfully shook the box.

"Open it," he said with an indulgent smile, sitting up, too.

"I'll be as spoiled as you with all these gifts. Is this part of your master plan to make sure no other man can compare?" she said.

"*Exactamente.*"

"Hmm. You're really making it tough on my future boyfriends."

"Good," he said with a big grin.

She opened the box and gasped when she saw the gift. It was a gold necklace with a diamond pendant and matching earrings. "Andres, this is too much."

"I want you to wear them when you come to DC in a couple of months."

"You want me to come see you then?" They'd discussed the trip but weren't sure they'd be able to get together because he'd only be in the country one day for the political event and then flying out the next day.

"Yes. Will you be traveling for work?"

"No, I should be able to make it."

"Good. I want you to wear this jewelry. For me? *Bueno?*"

"*Bueno.*" She leaned over and gave him a soft kiss. "You really are spoiling me."

"I can spoil you even more," he said.

Angela's shoulders sagged and she groaned. "Don't start." She scooted off the bed.

His response was a throaty chuckle. "I've told you before, quit your job and I'll take care of you."

"Ha, ha. Very funny."

"I'm serious," Andres said, as she padded over to the walk-in closet.

"I'm sure you are." She searched the rack for something to wear and removed a blazer, a pair of black pumps, a skirt, and a blouse. She grabbed underwear from one of the drawers.

"I am not kidding, Angela."

She ignored the firmer tone of his voice and stepped into the opulent bathroom. Gold fixtures and trim set against white marble glinted back at her. She put down her shoes and hung the clothes on the back of the door while a twist of...something filled her stomach.

Fear? Unease?

Andres hadn't brought up the topic since the trip to Isla de Vasquez, but she'd thought about it since then. It was not in her best interest to simply quit her job and become more available to him. Was he serious or kidding? What would she do with her time? How would they explain their arrangement? What would happen after the relationship was over? These were all the questions that plagued her.

Frowning to herself, she stepped into the shower and let lukewarm water cascade over her skin. When she was finished, she stepped out of the shower and removed a huge white towel from the warming rack.

She turned on the curling iron and after she finished getting dressed and put on her makeup, styled her long hair into waves that framed her face and dipped toward her breasts on either side. She then added her horn-rimmed glasses and was ready for another day of work.

Andres wore a pair of boxer briefs and stood before the table with a strip of bacon in his hand. His dark hair was still uncombed, and a spattering of hair on his face.

She stopped before him and twirled. "What do you think?"

A roguish grin covered his face. "You're like Superwoman. The glasses and the conservative dress are nice, but I know what's underneath." He tossed the bacon on the plate and approached.

Angela held a hand to his firm chest to hold him at bay. "Oh no, you don't. I'm leaving."

"Call in," he said, winding an arm around her waist.

"You know I can't."

His hands dropped away and irritation flickered across his face. "Why did you make a joke each time I brought up the possibility of you leaving your job and spending more time with me?"

She shifted. "Because I know you aren't serious."

"I am serious," Andres insisted.

"Sure you are."

"I'm not kidding, Angela. If I asked you now, would you?"

The conversation had taken an unexpected turn. She averted her gaze to the breakfast spread to avoid his penetrating look. She felt as if this were some kind of test.

"I can't quit my job. You know that."

"Why?"

"Because I'd rather not," Angela answered, laughing to make light of the situation. An argument was definitely pending.

"Why not?" he pushed.

"Why would I? So you can lord over me?"

The question was said in a half-joking manner, but his eyebrows snapped together. "Is that what you think? That I want to lord over you?" Before she could answer, he continued. "Maybe I'm just tired of this goddamn sneaking around. Every time I come see you, we stay in a hotel room."

"I thought you were fine with this arrangement."

"No, I'm not fine. I want to see you more often. I want to take you out. I want you to come with me to Estoria. I want to fly you to Paris for dinner or the Caribbean on vacation. I don't always want to be holed up in a hotel."

"So this is about you?" She marched across the room in search of her messenger bag and purse. Where had she dumped them last night when she arrived?

"No, it is not about me!" His voice got louder, his accent thicker.

She swung around. "I'm having fun, the way we are. I don't want or care about any of those things you mentioned."

"Well, maybe I do."

Angela's heart rate ticked up. "Why? Why are you suddenly so adamant that we move beyond what we have? Why are you trying to get me to quit my job? I don't want to lose myself and who I am. That's not me. I'm not arm candy."

"Then I'll give you a role in one of The Crown's companies."

"*Give* me? If I took a position in one of your companies, I'd want to earn it."

"I have every confidence in you. You did a great job with my firm. The COO was very pleased with your recommendations."

"Thank you, but that's not the point. What happens when you no longer want me around? I have to go job hunting again. Meanwhile, I've given up all the years I put in at Myers-Gomez? No thanks."

"Your role in my firm can be added to your résumé."

"I'm not interested." He was right, but she refused to budge. "Frankly, considering how busy we both are, I think we see each other plenty."

"It's barely enough."

"What are you saying?"

"I'm saying that one day, every few weeks won't be enough. Spending time together only when our schedules can coincide is not enough. One day you'll have to make a decision about how important this"—he gestured between them—"is to you." That sounded like a threat.

"And so will you."

Both of them stared at each other with heaving chests.

"I think I should go now." She spotted her messenger bag on the sofa and marched toward it, but Andres was faster.

He grabbed her arm. "I want more than a fling with you. Do you want me to say it?"

"Say what?"

"That I love you? That the reason I want you with me all the time is because I need you. *Te amo*. I love you, Angela. Does that make any difference?"

She hadn't expected him to say that, and the urgency in his voice called out to her. "I-I'm just not open to the arrangement you mentioned," she said in a quieter voice. "And I love you, too."

He pulled her into his arms and buried his fingers into her hair at the base of her neck. She held onto him tight.

"I know you're afraid of the media scrutiny. We can work through that or continue to keep our relationship a secret."

Angela rested her cheek against his bare chest. "We can't do that forever. Eventually, we'll have to go public if I move to Europe."

"So you're open to it?"

She hesitated. Was she?

Finally, she nodded. Though she downplayed its importance, she hated the distance between them and wanted to see him more often. More mornings waking up together and having breakfast. More dates. More touching. More kissing. More everything.

He kissed her temple. "I picked out some houses. Two in Spain and a villa in Estoria you might like."

"You've already started looking? You're serious about this."

"Yes, I am very serious."

She angled her head to get a better look at him. "I promise to think about it, but let's not spend the time we have left together fighting. We can figure out the details later. Can we just enjoy each other for now? *Please?*"

He smiled through his disappointment. "Okay, *mi amor*. But I'm not giving up. I can be very persuasive."

He gently kissed her on the lips, and then they sat down to eat breakfast.

16

Angela walked up the driveway of her parents' house. Her sister's red sedan was parked outside the garage, and she groaned inwardly. Three months had already passed since she moved in.

She entered the two-story home, the five bedrooms and six baths a downsized version of the home she'd grown up in. Her father's career in the music business had been very lucrative, and she'd wanted for nothing growing up in a house that was way too big for a family of three.

She found her mother in the open kitchen, stirring a pot of spaghetti sauce. Tessa Lipscomb was short, full-figured, and had a lovely pecan complexion. Her thick hair was currently covered by an Ankara print headwrap Angela had brought back for her from Africa.

"Hey, Mom."

Tessa turned. "Hey, honey."

Angela kissed her mother's cheek and then rested her hip against the island and watched her work. "What are you making for dinner?"

"This isn't for dinner. Your aunt asked me to make her some

spaghetti sauce. Once it's cool, I'll put it in some containers and take them over to her later. Want to ride with me?"

Angela shook her head. "Can't. I'm not staying long."

Her mother sprinkled herbs into the sauce. "What brings you by? You sounded a little odd on the phone." She covered the pot and turned down the heat.

"I have a lot on my mind."

Tessa faced her with worried eyes. "What's wrong?"

Angela didn't answer right away. She picked up an apple from the fruit bowl and tossed it back and forth in her hands. Finally she stopped and looked at her mother, who patiently waited for a response to her question.

"How did you know that Dad was the one?"

"Oh gosh, that's a tough question. When we met, he intimidated me. He was a high-ranking record executive, and I was a secretary who worked in the office. We got past that, but he came with so much baggage, we almost didn't get married. He had an ex-wife, a daughter who hated me, and of course, our racial differences. I wasn't sure if his white family would accept me or if my Black family would accept him. We had a lot of rocky moments."

"But you overcame them."

"Mhmm. Because we loved each other. But also because I let him know what I was willing to put up with. People are often unwilling to speak their minds, but honesty is the best policy in a relationship. Being upfront about what I was willing to tolerate helped. I told your father no more wild parties or cavorting around town with strange women all hours of the night and morning. I didn't want to live out west, so he bought us a house here. He changed a lot for me. When I saw what he was willing to give up, I became confident in his love and it made me believe we could work, no matter what problems came our way. Why do you ask?"

"Just wondering."

"No specific reason?"

Angela set the apple on the counter. "I'm seeing someone. It's serious, but it's not serious."

"I don't see how a relationship could be both. Anybody I know?" her mother asked.

"I'm not ready to talk about him yet, but he's become very important to me. More important than I anticipated. I think about him all the time, and I miss him so much when we're apart from each other."

The truth was, she'd become a little bit obsessed with Andres. Being away from him physically hurt, and her deep emotions terrified her. Feeling that way meant that she was prone to be impulsive and make an emotional decision instead of thinking clearly. She'd been down that road before and didn't want to make the same mistakes.

"I can't tell you what to do, but it sounds like he's not only important, you're in love with him."

Her chest tightened. "I am, and it scares me." Despite her flippant attitude during her conversation with Andres, she hadn't been completely turned off by the prospect of leaving her job and moving to Europe. The problem was, he didn't ask the question she'd wanted him to.

He wasn't talking about forever or a commitment in terms of marriage. Though marriage hadn't been on her mind before, she thought about it way more often now, and she only saw herself married to *him*. What he offered was something less permanent, less appealing, and riskier.

"Love is never easy. It's messy, complicated, and painful at times. But when you find the right one, it's absolutely worth it."

"You're saying that because you found the man of your dreams in Dad."

Her mother nodded. "True. But the way you talk about this mystery man—who I hope I get to meet very soon—sounds like he might be worth taking on whatever problems arise, too."

"Well, he definitely comes with a lot of baggage. The type of baggage that I'm not sure I'm ready to deal with, but I would consider dealing with it for him." She never thought she'd consider a life in the spotlight again, but she felt that for Andres, she'd be willing to do just about anything if it meant they could be together.

"Sounds like you've already made a decision."

Angela laughed. "Maybe. He has quite the big head, too, so I don't want to make him think that he's won me over yet."

Right then, her half-sister, Rebecca, dragged into the kitchen in flip-flops, sweats, and a T-shirt. Her blonde hair looked unkempt, as if she'd recently woken up, and she needed a trip to the hair-dresser as her black roots were showing more than an inch below the blonde on her head.

"Don't mind me. You can keep talking as if I'm not here," she said.

She opened the refrigerator, and Angela's gaze met her mother's. Neither one of them said a word as an awkward silence filled the room, which didn't seem to bother Rebecca. She whistled as she stood in front of the open refrigerator, searching the shelves.

Angela was fairly certain that her sister had come in there on purpose to disrupt their conversation and make them uncomfortable.

She swung away from the refrigerator. "Smells great in here. What's for dinner tonight?"

"This isn't for dinner. Your father mentioned that he might be coming home late, so you'll probably have to order in or cook a meal for yourself," Tessa replied.

"It's strange how you never cook when it's just you and me."

Unable to remain quiet, Angela said, "She doesn't have to. You have two hands."

Her mother shot her a warning look.

Rebecca smiled tightly. "I never learned to cook. My mother worked two jobs to support us while my father, *our* father, lived a luxurious life with his new wife and daughter. You, on the other hand, can probably make restaurant-worthy meals and were prob-ably trained by a chef, am I right?"

Angela's lips tightened.

"Angela," her mother warned.

Angela ignored her. "First of all, *our* father did what he was supposed to, but your mother squandered the money he gave her every month. If she hadn't, you wouldn't have struggled the way you did. Second, I don't give a shit what you think about me, but you leave my mother alone, do you hear me?"

"Or what?" Rebecca's eyes narrowed.

"Or I will make your life a living hell."

"You've already done that by being born." With a malevolent twist to her mouth, Rebecca sauntered out of the kitchen.

"Why did you do that?" her mother asked, eyes darting toward the open doorway.

"Why do you put up with her bullshit? You don't deserve that. Who the hell does she think she is, talking to you like that in your own home?"

"And who do you think you are, using that kind of language to me?"

Angela's shoulders slumped. "I'm sorry." She knew better than to curse in her mother's presence, but her sister brought out the worst in her.

Tessa smoothed her hand over the countertop. "Look, I know it's not the best situation—"

"At all."

"Let. Me. Finish."

Angela's shoulders slumped lower and she clamped her mouth shut.

"No, it's not the best situation, but she is his daughter, and he wants to help her. I'd do whatever it takes to help you if you needed me. So please, have a little more patience."

"I'm not as patient as you," Angela muttered.

Tessa's darker hand covered her fist on the counter. "Listen to me, you have a wonderful life, a great job, and now it seems a great man. Rebecca doesn't have any of that."

"Because she doesn't want to. She doesn't want to work. She'd prefer to wallow in self-pity and blame everyone else besides herself for her situation."

"For now."

"How much longer will this continue? She's over forty years old!"

"Shh." Tessa's eyes darted to the doorway again. "Some people take longer than others to find their way."

"You're being way too kind."

"I don't have much of a choice. She's in my life for the foreseeable future." Tessa went to the refrigerator and Angela watched her pour a glass of water. Her sympathy for her mother overrode her anger.

"I'm sorry, Mom."

Tessa shrugged. "It is what is. I can handle Rebecca. I don't care what she thinks about me or says to me. When you were little, I was determined that she leave you alone, and that remains the same. As long as she's not hurting you, that's all I care about."

"She can't hurt me," Angela said.

"Maybe. Let's keep it that way, okay?" Her mother glanced thoughtfully at the door. Then she smiled at her daughter. "Now, back to this mystery man. What are you going to do about him?"

Angela had come here seeking guidance, but in her heart, she already knew what she wanted to do. She had fallen in love with Andres. Crazy at it seemed, she'd probably fallen in love with him the first night they met. There were days when she no longer knew if she was coming or going. When the thought of losing him made her weak, her body slumped on the couch as she contemplated how to make the ache of needing him go away.

If their relationship was going to work long term, she'd have to give a little bit more than he did. He was limited by his position as a prince. She, however, had much more flexibility in her life and was now willing to take the leap into the unknown of this unique relationship and see where it would lead.

"He recently made me an offer, and…I think I'm going to take it."

17

Andres descended from the helicopter onto the helipad in the back courtyard of the palace grounds. His trip to the eastern tip of the island to meet with environmental engineers had taken longer than anticipated.

Based on the reports he'd reviewed, he'd wanted to visit the site himself. He had completely dismissed the idea of a casino-hotel and would inform his grandfather of his recommendation. In its place, he believed a marine park that incorporated an underwater observatory as a tourist attraction was a good way to diversify the nation's income-generating activities. His visit with the engineers confirmed there would be no environmental impact, and the funds generated could be used for conservation and preservation projects.

He walked briskly toward the back entrance and was mulling the pros and cons of his idea when his grandfather's secretary hurried toward him. She carried an electronic tablet against her bosom and wore a tailored dark blue dress and low-heeled shoes with stockings. The wind swept her short blonde hair across her eyes, and she brushed away the strands.

"Good afternoon, Your Highness," she said, and gave him a quick curtsy.

"Good afternoon, Agdalena. How can I help you?"

She fell into step beside him. "His Serene Highness would like to have a word with you in his office."

Andres came to a stop in the middle of the tiled hallway. Her harried expression gave him cause for concern. "Did he say why?"

It wasn't unusual for his grandfather to request his presence, but it was unusual for his grandfather to request his presence at the end of the day on a Friday. Though the palace was their primary residence, Andres rarely saw Prince Felipe nowadays, unless they were meeting to conduct palace business. That usually occurred earlier in the week.

"No, but it's very important, and he'd like to see you right away."

Her face gave no indication of whether or not the meeting was about good news or bad news. "All right. I'll go to my apartment and wash up a bit before I meet with him." Andres dismissed her with a nod and turned to walk away.

"He wants to meet with you now, Your Highness," Agdalena said, her voice a self-conscious squeak.

Andres turned slowly to face her. "It can't wait?"

She shook her head, squeezing the tablet harder against her chest. "No, Your Highness."

His eyebrows flew higher in surprise. "All right. I'll go there now. Thank you."

Andres headed in the opposite direction of the staircase that led to his apartment on the second floor. Frowning to himself, he wondered what could be so important that his grandfather couldn't wait a few minutes for him.

His footsteps echoed on the Italian tile and he nodded at staff that he encountered on the long walk to his grandfather's office.

The three-story palace had been originally built as a fortress on a hill to keep out enemy states but had gone through a series of renovations that modernized the interior. The high ceilings of yesteryear were painted with historic scenes that served as a reminder of the turbulent history the House of Vasquez had experienced throughout the years.

The sparkling blue Atlantic Ocean outside the arched windows made him long for the next time he'd see Angela again. So far they'd managed to see each other every two to three weeks and spent a lot of time on the phone when they couldn't.

Andres entered the office. "Hello, Grandfather. You wanted to see me?"

Felipe turned away from the window and the busy harbor where ferries shuttled residents and visitors back and forth to mainland Europe.

"Yes, I did. Care to sit?" He inclined his head toward one of the chairs.

"I'd rather stand," Andres said, somehow certain he should remain on his feet for this conversation.

Felipe studied his hands for a moment, and Andres remained silently waiting for him to explain why he'd been summoned.

"I'm not getting any younger," Felipe began, looking up at Andres. "I have made a decision. In one year I will abdicate the throne."

"Abdicate?" Andres repeated in shock. He'd fully expected his grandfather to continue as the country's ruler for years to come, despite his age.

"Yes, and I want *you* to succeed me on the throne."

What! This decision was completely unexpected.

"There is no one better suited than you. Over the past few years, you've handled every task I've handed you with the finesse and skill our people expect from a future ruler."

Shocked, Andres remained silent.

Perhaps he'd done too well, because he hadn't expected his grandfather to appoint him as the next head of state. His father should have been the next in line, but because he was unfit and exiled, Felipe had the right to appoint his successor, and Andres had thought for sure his grandfather would choose an older member of the family.

"What about your nephew, Juan the Viscount of Guzman? He would be better suited than me." While he had reservations about his cousin's preparedness for the role, he'd expected his grandfather to choose him. He'd served the country faithfully for years and could surely become an excellent ruler with good support and the passage of time. If not him, then another family member.

Felipe shook his head gravely. "He is not suitable, in my opinion. His decision-making is lacking, and he has no charisma. Since your father, my own son, is out of the question..." He grimaced. "I choose you." His blue eyes, dulled with age as his vision declined, brightened somewhat as he stared directly at Andres.

Andres shook his head. "No, Grandfather. I don't think I'm ready."

"You are as ready as you will ever be. In October you will be thirty years old, two years older than I was when I took the throne. I have every confidence in you."

Silence fell in the room as Andres rummaged through his mind for more excuses that would get him out of the responsibility that loomed in the near future.

His stomach became as tight as a ball of yarn. "Grandfather..." he started, unsure of his argument but certain he must lodge one.

"The weekend of your thirtieth birthday celebration, I will make the announcement that you will succeed me to the throne and let our citizens know the date I will abdicate in July of next year. Then we will simply have to get the endorsement of the National Council, which I fully expect we will once the members vote."

"This is so sudden."

"We don't have any choice. Nature, it seems, has chosen to be unkind to me in my old age." Felipe slowly shook his head, and Andres waited on tenterhooks for him to continue. "My doctors have informed me that I'm in the early stages of Alzheimer's."

All the air left the room. Felipe's grave face wrenched at Andres's heart. That diagnosis explained so much—the forgetfulness, the odd behavior.

"They have given me a year, maybe two if I'm lucky, before my condition becomes more noticeable. It's already progressed past my comfort level. I lose things. The other day I couldn't do simple arithmetic. My condition will only get worse, so there's no point in delay. You know what that means, of course. You must choose a wife, a woman of noble birth who can bear you the children that will continue our lineage. *Not* a woman with whom you have a fling that will lead nowhere."

Andres felt his stomach churn. He was speaking about Angela.

His grandfather had never approved of their relationship, one that had lasted longer than any of his most recent ones. She was American and a commoner. Felipe would have much preferred that he get serious about someone from Europe, from the long list of eligible nobility across the continent. A princess, a countess. Anyone else but a woman who didn't have the right background and hadn't been through the training and grooming necessary to become the mother of future princes and princesses.

Felipe had no doubt expected their relationship to last only a short time, but there was no end in sight. Until today. Until he had essentially given Andres notice that he should end their affair to pick a bride and prepare for his role as ruler of Estoria.

"There is no law that says I have to marry a woman of noble birth."

His grandfather looked at him askance. "It is best. Are you thinking about the woman you're seeing? I hope not, because she is not prepared."

"Then *I* will prepare her."

"You know as well as I do that she wants no part of this." He waved his hand at the room. "You told me so yourself. *She* is the one who has insisted that you keep your relationship secret. She is an independent and career-driven woman. Do you really think she would give up her lifestyle for you? For the limitations you must live under and the protocol you must succumb to as the reigning monarch?"

Andres ran a hand over his head and stepped away, unable to meet his gaze and accept the lash of his words.

"Choose a woman from Spain or the United Kingdom or Sweden. Such an alliance would be beneficial for us. She won't be accepted. You know she won't fit in."

The hairs on the back of Andres's neck rose. What did that vague comment mean? Was he referring to her biracial heritage?

He swung around. "And what the hell does that mean?"

"Watch your tone." Felipe's stooped shoulders straightened fractionally. "This is not up for debate. It is time for you to end your affair with this woman—"

"Her name is Angela," Andres said through clenched teeth. He regretted ever sharing his strong feelings for her with his grandfather.

"Think about our future. You know what happens if you do not marry."

Public and political unrest would ensue.

Despite their valiant efforts, Estoria had been annexed by the Portuguese for decades in the early years of its founding. They'd finally gotten their freedom by paying a handsome sum to the Portuguese monarchy and allying themselves with bigger, more powerful countries ruled by a king or queen. As such, they'd called their own rulers princes and princesses, thus making them a principality.

Their freedom did not come without a catch, however. According to the agreement they had signed, any ruler who ascends the throne must be married and produce a hereditary, legitimate heir to the throne within two years. If not, a re-annexation would result, dissolving Estoria's monarchy and returning the country and all its assets to Portugal.

"You know what you must do. Do it." Felipe returned his attention to the scene outside the window, ending the conversation.

Andres couldn't remember the last time he'd received a hug from his grandfather. Felipe was not an affectionate man, yet Andres knew he loved him and understood that love went beyond mere physical touch. One's actions conveyed love, and his grand-father had demonstrated many times how much Andres meant to him.

He'd cast out his own son and raised Andres as his own. He'd educated him in the ways of royal protocol, sent him to the best schools, and given him the type of worldly advice that should have come from his own father. Now, he was asking him to continue the name of the House of Vasquez—which would have been an honor, had it not come with the burden of losing the woman he loved.

Among the palace staff, there were people who completed the most mundane of tasks, such as fetching a cup of coffee. Or they performed the most dire, unselfish act—like the security guards willing to die for them. In exchange, all he was being asked to do was lead, from a golden throne in a palace on a hill.

But he couldn't think of anything but Angela and what that announcement would mean for their future.

A haze of misery covered him from head to toe, and he left the office without speaking another word. Prince Felipe had spoken. As his grandfather and prince, he must be obeyed.

18

A ngela smiled at the attendant whose firm hand rested beneath hers as he helped her out of the limousine.

"Have a good evening, ma'am," he said.

"Thank you," she replied.

She made her way to the brightly lit front door of the Smithsonian Castle, where a female attendant welcomed her in with a sweep of her hand.

The fall event by billionaire Damon Steed was well attended every year. Top U.S. political figures and foreign dignitaries were there tonight, all dressed in fine gowns and tuxedos.

Her invite had come through her best friend, Dahlia, but she was there to meet Andres. He'd flown her to DC and also provided the clothes she wore, a shimmering gold dress with a striped shawl that was thrown around her shoulders. The shoes and matching gold clutch were also part of the ensemble that he had forwarded to her.

She had to give it to him, he'd done a good job—or whomever he'd hired to pick out the clothes for this evening. She'd never considered herself the type to have a man tell her what to wear, but she'd found herself willing to do for Andres a lot of things she didn't normally do. And despite being independent, she appreciated his gifts and desire to spoil her. Her heart beat rapidly in anticipation of seeing him. She couldn't wait to tell him, in person, that she was willing to move to Europe so they could spend more time together. And maybe, just maybe, she could eventually work up the nerve to be in the spotlight.

Baby steps…

A white-gloved attendant caught her eye and motioned for her to enter the Great Hall where the main festivities were taking place. The Great Hall was an impressive two-story space with tall windows and colossal arched columns.

She stepped in and cast her gaze around. She and Andres were going to pretend they didn't know each other, but she couldn't help but search for him.

Finally, she saw him, not too far from where she stood, seated with a group of men around a table. Her gaze took him in, holding court while the other men practically hung on his every word.

His eyes met hers and sent the pulse at the base of her throat into a frenzy.

He was absolutely breathtaking. His black hair was swept away from his face, but later when they made love, that one errant curl would fall out of place across his forehead, and she'd take pleasure in pushing it back into place with the run of her fingers.

She expected some acknowledgement from him. A small lift of the corner of his mouth perhaps, or even letting his gaze sweep down her body in approval the way he often did. Instead, his face remained neutral and his gaze moved away from hers.

He continued his conversation, and for a moment Angela was thrown. They'd agreed to pretend they didn't know each other, but she still felt dismissed.

Was something wrong? Did he not like what he saw? Did—

She halted the negative thoughts, certain she was reading too much into his lack of reaction, and made her way across the floor. She stopped one of the waiters and took a glass of white wine from him, offering a faint smile as she did so. She should not be drinking on an empty stomach, but she needed something to hold in her hand while amongst all these very important people.

"Hey, stranger," came a whisper in her ear.

Before Angela turned around, a smile swept across her face at the familiar voice of her best friend.

Immediately, both women enveloped each other in one-armed hugs because they each held a glass in their hand. Angela had known Dahlia since college, and too long had passed since they'd been able to see each other in person. She missed her bestie so much.

Dahlia stepped back and looked her up and down, one eyebrow raised. "You look amazing." Her voice lowered. "Andres?"

"Of course." Angela made good money in her career, but not enough to warrant spending the kind of money this one-of-a-kind dress, the accessories, and the diamond jewelry had certainly cost.

"He's already here. Have you seen him?" Dahlia asked. She sipped a glass of water with a lemon wedge floating inside it.

She looked incredible with her wavy dark hair swept up into a neat style and wore a purple, floor-length gown with a beaded bodice and trumpet sleeves. At five months pregnant with her second child, her belly dominated the front of the dress more than it did around the same time with her first baby. Being pregnant had made her face rounder and given her dark brown skin a healthy glow.

"I saw him when I came in," Angela replied.

"Come on, let's go over here. My feet are killing me." Dahlia led the way to a couple of unoccupied chairs and lowered into one. "Whew, I thought no one would ever get up so I could sit down."

Crossing her legs, Angela grinned and let the shawl drop to the bend in her elbows. "All you have to do is play the pregnancy card and people will let you sit."

"I know." Dahlia shifted in the chair, trying to get comfortable. "I just try not to do it if I don't have to."

"How is my godson?" Angela asked, referring to Dahlia's first-born, Noel.

"Learning a lot, picking up the language, and doing a great job at assimilating. Much better than his mother."

"Oh, come on. We both know that's not true. Things may have been difficult in the beginning, but you've come a long way in a short time."

Dahlia smiled gratefully. "It's been quite the adventure," she said.

They took a moment to watch the people walking around. Angela spotted a famous actor and the Senate Majority Leader with his wife.

"What about you and Andres?" Dahlia asked lightly.

Angela shrugged. "We're still going strong."

Dahlia leaned closer and lowered her voice. "Kofi thinks Andres is crazy about you. He's never seen him this way over a woman, and he says it's very unusual that Andres is so willing to make concessions where *he* comes to *you*."

"Well, that's not the case tonight. I came to him."

"Only because he's flying back to Estoria tomorrow. Otherwise, he would have met you in Atlanta."

Angela couldn't help but grin. He had been very accommodating ever since they started seeing each other. He'd agreed to keep their relationship quiet, which wasn't easy. And arriving to events separately and taking the back entrance whenever they dined together had worked so far.

Her mother had told her she was willing to sacrifice to be with her father because he'd changed for her. Andres had clearly changed for Angela and shown how much he cared for her and enjoyed her company.

"I'm lucky, I guess."

"Lucky, or you have that man wrapped around your finger."

"I'd hardly say that's the reason," Angela said, though the idea excited her, despite his tepid response tonight.

Kofi, Dahlia's husband, strolled over in a tuxedo. Strong-jawed with a circle beard and a regal bearing, he was a handsome man who looked every bit the prince he was.

"Angela, good to see you. You look lovely this evening, though not as lovely as my wife," he added, his unusual accent a mixture of the three languages he spoke—French, English, and his tribal tongue, Mbutu.

"Lucky save. You mean your fat wife?" Dahlia said.

"My beautifully pregnant wife," he said with a smile. "I hate to interrupt, but there's someone I need Dahlia to meet. Do you mind?"

"Not at all," Angela replied. "In fact, I'll take this opportunity to do a little mingling, which includes making a beeline for the refreshments table. I didn't eat before coming here, so I'm a little bit hungry."

Kofi helped Angela from the chair and then extended his hand to Dahlia and eased her up, as well.

"Duty calls," Dahlia said, sounding disappointed. "We have to talk before you leave tonight, once we get through with our official business."

"Definitely."

They walked away, and Angela sidled over to the refreshments.

ANDRES STRUGGLED NOT to look in Angela's direction for the umpteenth time since her arrival and failed miserably. He had practically dropped out of the conversation with his acquaintances, sneaking glances each time the guests parted and he caught a good glimpse of her. The dress fit perfectly, and the color made her tawny skin glimmer like the gold beads sewn into the fabric.

She wore her hair pinned up with a gold clip that he knew from past experience he could easily undo and release her soft hair into his waiting hands. She looked amazing, which would make what he had to do tonight even more difficult. He'd thought talking to her in person was best, but now he wasn't so sure.

From the moment they met, he'd known she was the one. Yet he hadn't anticipated this—this crushing squeeze of his heart at the thought of letting her go.

He took a sip of his vodka and then smiled absently when the group of men erupted into laughter. He had no idea what they were talking about or what the joke was.

As a man used to having anything he wanted, he had to accept that he could never have Angela. Not really. The fate of his country depended on his ability to act, and his grandfather would never approve his marriage to her. Even if he did, she had no desire to live her life in the public eye.

Now he had to tell her their relationship was over. But how could he, when all he wanted to do was get her naked and claim that mouth that haunted him every time they were apart?

19

Angela was in the process of filling up her plate when a male voice with a charming Southern accent said beside her, "I like a woman who has a hearty appetite."

She swung her gaze to the right and saw a distinguished-looking gentleman with gray hairs at his left temple and an easy-going smile.

"That's not the best comment to make to someone you just met," she said.

He chuckled softly. "As soon as the sentence left my mouth, I knew I had made a mistake, but my opinion still stands." His gaze swept over her. "I'm Sen. Charles Radcliffe, from the great state of South Carolina."

Angela set down her plate and shook his hand. "Angela Lipscomb. From the great state of Georgia." She grinned.

"Something tells me you're not in government."

"I'm not. I'm a management consultant. I received a special invitation, as a guest of the Zamibian royal family."

"My, my, you know some people in high places. And a management consultant, you said? Hm, I think I need some managing." His eyes twinkled at her.

If she were into older men, she could definitely go for this guy.

Some women might find him off-putting, but he had a certain charm.

"I consult for companies, not individuals."

"I have a company," he said.

"Are you in need of a consultant?"

"I could be. If it meant I got to spend more time with you."

"Senator Radcliffe, I'm flattered, but I'm not in the habit of picking up men at formal events."

The smile didn't leave his face. "Please, call me Charles. I think by the end of the night, you and I are going to know each other much better."

From that moment on, Angela spent her time in conversation with the senator who, it turned out, really did own a company. She gave him some advice, but they mostly talked about other topics. Eventually, a representative from California joined them and the three migrated to four-chair seating around a small round table.

They resumed chatting, this time about vacation spots. Because she'd done a lot of traveling for work, domestic and international, Angela gave them recommendations for places she'd visited, admitting her affinity for Asia, the cultures, foods, and people.

She was enjoying herself immensely when Senator Radcliffe's gaze settled over her right shoulder. Without him saying a word, she knew who was on the approach. In a short time, she'd become attuned to his presence, as if they were two parts of a whole, magnetically drawn to each other no matter where they were.

Her body tightened in anticipation.

"Senator Radcliffe, Representative Dow." The sound of his voice always got her a little excited.

Both politicians stood, extending their hands, and Angela turned to face Andres but remained seated.

"Prince Andres, it's good to see you." The three men shook hands before Andres looked down at her.

"And you are…Angela, correct? We met at Prince Kofi of Zamibia's wedding." He extended a hand.

What was he doing?

"That's correct." Angela stood and shook his hand. His clasp was warm and the handshake firm.

"If I recall, you're a consultant, aren't you?"

"Yes, that's correct."

"I'm in need of a consultant, as a matter of fact."

"You are?"

He looked at the other two men. "Gentlemen, do you mind if I borrow her?"

Sen. Radcliffe looked disappointed, but he bowed in acquiescence. "Go right ahead, Prince Andres. Ms. Lipscomb, it was nice to meet you. I hope we'll have the pleasure of speaking again before you leave."

He took her hand and kissed the back of it. The representative shook her hand and both men walked away.

"Were you flirting with those men to get under my skin?" Andres asked.

"Maybe a little," she teased.

"It worked," he said grimly.

She'd never seen him like this. He'd expressed jealousy before, but he hadn't cracked a smile at her teasing words.

"I thought we weren't supposed to talk to each other or let anyone know that we knew each other," Angela said.

"Change of plans. Let's get out of here." He seemed restless, agitated.

"Now?"

"Yes."

"It's early. Why so sudden?"

"Because I'm hard from the thought of fucking you and making them watch, and if I have to witness one more man drool over you I'm going to lose my goddamn mind."

She glanced around the room, checking to make sure no one nearby had heard him. In private, there were times when he used raw, unfiltered language, but he'd never spoken to her in public in this way. Those types of conversations were reserved for their times alone.

Like the times he took control in the bedroom.

On your knees.

She swallowed at the recollection of his voice—commanding, guttural. She tasted his salty flavor and relived the weight of him in her mouth. She heard the dirty talk as he gripped her hair and held her in place, his eyes glittering down at her from above.

But this was more than dirty talk. She once again had the distinct impression that he was upset.

"Is something wrong?" she asked, studying him. She couldn't shake the unease and needed his reassurance.

His expression gave nothing away. "I'm fine. I want you. That's why you're here."

Her breath hitched. The words stung, even more so since they'd expressed their love for each other the last time. Maybe he was still a bit resentful that she'd refused his offer to move to Europe.

"All right," she said quietly because she couldn't think of any other answer.

"I'm staying at the Winthrop on Pennsylvania Avenue." He glanced at his watch, the same Cartier timepiece studded with diamonds that he'd worn the night they met. "I'm leaving now. Go to the valet stand in fifteen minutes. The limo will be waiting for you."

She nodded, still unsure of his present mood, but she wanted him, too. Later, they could get to the bottom of his foul attitude. Probably something to do with his country. Maybe he'd run into a problem with his environmental plans. He'd confided in her in the past. Perhaps a change of venue would make the difference.

"I'll see you soon," he said, and marched away.

20

"Hello, Ollie," Angela said to the tall and wiry blond. Despite his small frame, he exuded strength.

"Hello, Ms. Lipscomb."

The guard helped her from the car, and she followed him to the elevator. They took it to one of the top floors and walked down the quiet hallway to a door where a large man with a thick neck stood guard and only granted them a cursory glance. Ollie knocked twice, but instead of waiting for someone to let them in, he entered and motioned for her to precede him. She walked into the suite, which was similar to the one Andres had rented in Atlanta, with hardwood floors and huge windows that looked out onto the street.

"Prince Andres will be with you shortly," Ollie said. Then he backed out and closed the door.

Angela walked farther into the room, assessing the interior, decorated with chairs covered in floral and striped prints. Two coffee tables rested between three sofas in the shape of a U, and wooden stands held vases of fresh flowers and potted plants.

She placed her clutch and shawl on one of the sofas and made her way over to the windows. The view from up here was spectacular, but she didn't expect anything less from Andres.

She knew when he entered the room, and then his reflection appeared in the glass. He only wore the white shirt and dark slacks from his tuxedo.

She didn't move, and he slipped his arms around her waist and pressed his face into the side of her neck. With a sigh, she melted back against him, her body sagging into the familiar warmth of his.

God, she missed him. She wanted him everywhere. Between her legs. On top of her. His hands were beautiful. His mouth was beautiful. Even the way he frowned evoked sexy thoughts because she imagined that same frown represented concentration as he thrust into her.

His arms tightened. She arched her neck, and his lips traced the curve as he dropped moist kisses onto her skin.

"Has any other man touched you since we've been together?"

Angela moaned. "No."

"Has any other man kissed you?" His tongue swept the shell of her ear.

She shivered. "No." She turned and slipped her arms around his torso. "I belong to the prince of Estoria."

His nostrils flared, and he cupped her face in his long-fingered hands. "Yes, you are mine." He practically growled the words as his blue eyes filled with a fierce light.

She was making a joke, but she didn't get the sense that he was joking right now.

He pressed his hands against the glass, making it impossible for her to get away from him.

"Take off your panties."

"You're so impatient. You can't wait?" she teased.

"With you, no. Take them off."

She made direct eye contact. "I'm not wearing any."

He froze. "You came to the event with no…" The words trailed off, as if he couldn't finish the thought.

Slowly, she pulled at her dress, drawing the hem higher. Andres watched with fascination until she'd gathered the fabric in such a way, the hemline was pulled up past her hips and exposed her nakedness.

He didn't move at first, his shallow breaths the only indication that he paid attention to her wanton display. Then he dropped to his knees, and she closed her eyes when his whole mouth closed over the arch between her thighs.

He lifted one leg over his shoulder and angled his mouth to taste deeper, his tongue dipping into the moist flesh and then burrowing into her wet channel. Angela moaned, eyes closed, pleasure holding her captive against the cool glass. She undulated her hips as he licked and sucked.

"Don't stop, Andres. Please." She dropped the dress and grabbed her breasts, squeezing them together and playing with the nipples.

Under her dress, his tongue swept across her wet lips and sucked her swollen clit. But then he abruptly stopped, stood, and simply looked down at her.

She wound her arms around his neck. "I want to come. Please, Andres."

He lifted her in his arms, took her to the bedroom, and placed her in the bed. He stripped the clothes from her body and from his and then climbed in after her.

He claimed between her legs again and kissed her center until she came all over his mouth with a hoarse cry. She clawed the sheets as her body quivered in the aftermath. Dizzy and spent, she scooted backward in an effort to escape.

But Andres wasn't having it. His hands tightened on her thighs.

"I'm not done. You begged me to come," he growled over her wet flesh.

He dragged her back to his mouth and forced her legs wider. He took control and there was nothing she could do but accept the sensual assault. Accept the way that he laved her wet core and accept that he wouldn't stop until he was satisfied. Grabbing onto his hair, she closed her eyes and savored how his stiff tongue roamed the delicate folds. He knew just what to do and seemed intent on literally driving her insane with pleasure.

With a long, dragging suck, he pulled another bone-melting orgasm from the depths of her body. She rocked under the force of climactic shock and was breathless and panting when he finally released her.

He crawled up the bed and put his soft mouth over a hard, aching nipple. He sucked at the same time his hands rubbed over her belly and the curve of her hips.

Angela smoothed her hands over his back as she arched deeper into his caresses.

"Now," he muttered.

He seared their bodies together with unexpected urgency. God, how she loved the sensation when he first entered her. Her fingernails sank into his shoulders, and then he was lifting her hips off the bed to get in deeper.

"Andres," she whimpered.

He kissed her cheeks and her neck. Squeezed her breasts and tugged on her nipples. She came again, crying out, her hips bouncing up and down as she lost control. Her cry triggered a groan and more powerful pumping from him. As she quivered around his length, his erratic, borderline violent thrusts signaled that he neared climax.

Burying his face in her neck, he gripped her hips and finally collapsed on top of her.

EYES STILL CLOSED, Angela reached blindly across the bed, expecting to find Andres's body. Her arm encountered a cool sheet and an empty mattress instead.

How long had she been asleep?

She shoved her thick hair from her face and her eyes fluttered open. Rising onto her elbows, she let her pupils get accustomed to the dim light.

Andres wasn't in the bathroom, either. There was no light under the door. Where was he?

She sat all the way up and swung her legs off the side of the bed, scouring the floor for an article of clothing to throw over her naked body. She picked up his discarded white shirt and pushed her arms through the long sleeves. His scent filled her nostrils, and she pressed her nose into the collar and took a big whiff.

Treading quietly, she walked into the living room and found Andres seated on the sofa in a white hotel robe, staring out a window. He held a tumbler of clear liquid on one thigh. His hair was tousled after their lovemaking, and she smiled, amused that she'd been the one to give him that endearing, disheveled look.

His stillness made her pause. He was frowning, in such deep thought he hadn't noticed she'd entered the room. There was definitely something wrong with him, and it was time to get to the bottom of it.

She moved forward again, and he suddenly glanced in her direction.

"You're up," he said.

"Yes. And you look like you've been up for a while." Angela sat down beside him and folded one leg beneath her. She brushed her fingertips through his dark hair. "What's going on? Something's obviously on your mind. Talk to me. You know you can tell me anything."

"I can?"

Surprised by his skepticism, she withdrew her hand and rested it on the back of the sofa. "Of course. You've trusted me in the past. Is there some problem with Estoria?"

While she couldn't fully understand the extent of his duties, she knew his position as prince could be a demanding one.

"I don't have a lot of time…" His words trailed off as he roughly shoved his fingers through his hair, further disturbing the strands.

"Time for what?" Her chest tightened. Something was very, very wrong.

"Nothing," he replied irritably. He stood and stalked over to the bar.

"It's not nothing, Andres."

He didn't reply. As if he hadn't set a half-full glass on the bar top, he poured himself another vodka, this time on the rocks. He took a sip and then dropped his hand. The bottom of the glass hit the bar with a loud bang.

She walked over to him and stood several feet away. "What is it?"

His jaw tightened and the seconds stretched by as he gazed down into the clear liquid. Finally, he looked at her. "It's my grandfather," he said solemnly.

"Is there something wrong with Prince Felipe?"

"As you know, he hasn't been well. He's gotten more forgetful in his old age and the doctors told him he has Alzheimer's."

"Oh no, I'm sorry." She stepped closer and rubbed his back.

No wonder he was so distracted. He and his grandfather were very close, and he was bound to face some trying times as the disease progressed.

"That's not all," Andres said in a grim tone. He kept his back turned to her and his head bowed. "He's made a decision about the successor to the throne."

Angela became very still. "You," she said softly.

"Yes."

Prince Felipe had skipped over other family members Andres had been certain he'd choose.

"What does this mean?" Angela squeaked.

His voice lowered. "Due to my grandfather's age and declining health, it means…" He straightened his shoulders. "More work for me, less time traveling, and next year I will ascend the throne."

Angela stood uncertainly. There were more bad news. She knew it.

Andres finally faced her, and their eyes locked. "And I must find a wife."

21

No.

The shock of his declaration rammed into Angela with unexpected force.

"You're going to marry someone else?" She knew the answer but needed him to say it.

"Yes." That single word decimated her.

"You told me you loved me and now you're going to marry someone else?"

"Angela, I don't have a choice. Do you really think I want to do this?"

She wasn't being fair. She was judging him too harshly, but she couldn't help it.

"How much time do we have?" she asked, her lips so numb she found it difficult to speak.

"Our time is at an end. My grandfather has already prepared a list of recommended brides for me to choose from. He will abdicate in July of next year, at which time I will become the ruling monarch of my country. The announcement will be made in a couple of weeks."

Angela blinked. "So soon? When did you find out?"

"Two weeks ago."

"Wait a minute, and you still met me tonight?"

"We'd already made plans. I wanted to see you."

"What? How could you, Andres? So you screwed me even though you knew you had this news to tell me? What was all this? The perfect kiss goodbye?" She felt sick.

"Do you think this was easy for me? We are two people from completely different backgrounds and completely different countries who met in a foreign country at a wedding and have spent an incredible time getting to know each other. So incredible I cannot think of anyone else but you. Do you have any idea how hard it is not to touch you right now? To not push you back against that glass and tear off my shirt so I can have you one more time?"

"Is that supposed to be a compliment? Somehow that just makes what you've done worse." Was that all she was to him? A body to use? "You're despicable. You should have told me."

"Does it really matter to you? You're an independent woman. You don't care about such things like marriage," he grated.

She winced. The words sounded like an indictment, but Andres had been slowly chipping away at her autonomy. When he came to Atlanta, she dropped everything. Friends and family were put on the back burner so she could spend as much time with him as possible.

"So you decide to punish me because I wouldn't go along with your plans, *Your Royal Highness*?"

"You wanted to be here, and I wanted to tell you the truth, in person. But when we came upstairs, you were so…ready." A flash of heat entered his eyes. "I couldn't help myself."

Her cheeks warmed. He truly did look ready to push her against the glass, and if she didn't know the truth, she would have let him. They'd spend the rest of their time together making love, laughing, and talking in earnest the way they always did. She'd tell him she was ready to uproot her life for him and be the kind of woman she never thought she was. None of that would happen now.

"Lucky for us, we both got the sex out of our system," she said.

"Our relationship doesn't have to end. We can continue seeing each other."

"Oh really? Excuse me if I don't jump at the chance to continue being with you while you plan your wedding to another woman." She laughed bitterly. "Or are you making me a different offer? You get married and I continue to be your American side piece? Was that the idea? Be a whore for you the way your grandfather had a whore?"

Color tinged his high cheekbones.

"I should slap you but I don't want to expel the energy," she said.

Angela marched by him, intending to go to the bedroom, but he caught her forearm and tugged her back around to look at him.

She yanked her arm away and glared at him with enough heat to pulverize granite into dust. "Don't you dare touch me." Her voice quivered, but it wasn't just with anger. She was hurt. More devastated than she could have ever imagined, and she couldn't let him know the extent of her pain, how it gnawed at her insides like acid on steroids.

"This is not how I wanted our relationship to end," he said.

"Then you should have handled the situation better." She stormed into the bedroom, blinking back tears.

She'd known the relationship would end at some point, but losing him—especially in this way, was so devastating. She couldn't let him know the extent of her pain. She couldn't let him know that she was dying inside.

The few weeks between their meetings had become long and untenable. How could she possibly deal with a separation that yawned in front of her like a wide open chasm with no end in sight?

Andres's firm hands landed on her hips and he spun her around.

"I need you," he muttered in a husky voice.

She shoved him, and he pushed her onto the bed and fell on top of her.

"If you think—"

"I don't have to think, I know. You belong to me, Angela. You said so yourself."

He pinned her wrists above her head and his mouth landed on hers with bruising intensity. She twisted against him, kneeing him in the side, but he continued undeterred. One hand squeezed her breast and her traitorous nipple became a turgid, pointed peak.

He pressed kisses against her neck and then pulled aside the shirt to fasten his mouth over the same breast. She twisted against him again, fighting her own body's will to succumb to him.

"Andres," she moaned.

"I am here," he whispered. He licked her nipple and then released her wrists to slide his other hand between her legs.

She closed her eyes, biting down on her lip as he stroked her with precision. Her head was swimming. The sensations he evoked threatened to overwhelm her.

He released the belt on the robe and it fell open, exposing the magnificence of his hard shaft. She bit down harder on her lip as her body experienced a wrenching ache to have him enter her.

She rested her fists on his shoulders. She should push him away, but couldn't. Just one more time. She needed him one more time.

She would never be able to touch him again. These were their last moments together, and she didn't want to waste a single second. This wasn't about him. *She* wanted it. She could say goodbye any way she wanted, and this was the way she chose.

The thought of losing him scalded her insides, but she dragged his mouth down to hers and kissed him hungrily, taking her fill. Their bodies rubbed against each other, turning her wet and eager for his possession. She reached between them and circled his hard shaft. He groaned her name, as if he could barely stand to be touched. He kissed her neck, her collarbone, and the swells of her breasts, his breathing harsh as she continued to stroke him.

She shifted so that the tip of him nudged the entrance to her body, and he shoved into her without further prompting, fastening his lips on her neck as he did so. Angela squeezed her eyes shut, giving herself over to the exquisite sensation of him thrusting hard and slow, in and out, each movement of his body catapulting her toward the edge.

She couldn't stop groaning. He felt so good. He felt like heaven. She never wanted him to stop.

ANDRES PICKED up the phone and dialed. "I'm ready," he said and hung up.

He walked over to the table and poured himself a glass of orange juice but ignored the pastries, fruit, and eggs on the table. He had no appetite. In a few minutes, his driver would be waiting downstairs to take him to the airport for the flight back to Estoria. In a couple of weeks, his grandfather would announce his decision to abdicate, and then all eyes would be on Andres more than ever.

His body hardened as he recalled mere hours before, when he and Angela lay in bed together. He'd tried to slake his lust and get her out of his system, and they'd essentially worn each other out during the night and into the morning. When she slipped from his arms at dawn, he knew he could no longer hold onto her.

She hardly looked at him and left without even a word of good-bye. As if she couldn't bear to look at him. He knew she enjoyed their lovemaking and suspected that she resented him for using her body's own desires against her.

Bitterness festered in his chest, and he laughed sourly at how much his life had changed in a short period. A wave of anguish and anger came to life in a volcanic rush. He tossed the glass of juice across the room. It shattered against the wall, spattering orange across the wallpaper and down onto the hardwood floor.

Mierda. "Forget her."

He had responsibilities. He *had* to forget her. And that's exactly what he intended to do.

22

"Make sure the old man next door doesn't see you," Andres said.

Ollie nodded. He climbed out of the SUV and disappeared into the night.

Andres let his head fall back against the seat and raked shaky fingers through his hair. Forgetting about Angela didn't last. He kept tabs on her and he shouldn't have. He shouldn't be *here*. But ever since they broke up, he'd felt lost. The finality of their split weighed heavy on his mind.

Then to find out that she was already seeing someone, a jealous rage sank its claws into him. He wanted her to explain how she could move on so quickly when he hadn't had a good night's sleep since they split two weeks ago in DC. If she'd brought that man home or gone to his house, he didn't know what he would have done. Something he would have regretted later but in the moment would have seemed perfectly reasonable in the face of his right-eous anger.

Ollie tapped lightly on the car window and Andres joined him outside.

"The back door is open."

"Good. I'll be right back."

"Your Highness…"

"I'll be fine. I'm only going two blocks away, and I know how to reach you." Andres held up his left hand and showed him the Cartier watch which was outfitted with a sophisticated alert mechanism. When he pressed and held down the face for two seconds, the watch sent an emergency signal to his security team.

"Very well, sir." Ollie stepped back.

Feeling a little bit like a criminal, Andres went around to the back of Angela's house and entered the door Ollie had left open for him. He locked it and waited for his eyes to adjust to the darkness. Then he walked through the house and climbed the stairs. He didn't hear any sounds until he reached the top level. She was in the bathroom.

He sat down on the bed and waited, while memories of the first time they'd made love in this very bed came back to him in vivid detail. Her writhing body beneath his. The way she whispered his name in a husky plea.

The bathroom door snicked open and Angela came out with a blue towel wrapped around her torso and her damp hair showing its natural wave pattern. She padded barefoot over to the dresser and pulled open one of the drawers.

"Angela."

She swung around with a little cry and clutched her chest. "Andres! How…how did you get into my house?" Her eyes darted around the room as if she were searching for someone else.

"I needed to see you."

She gave a short laugh. "Oh, well that makes it perfectly fine for you to break into my home."

"I was worried you wouldn't let me in if I came to the front door."

"You were absolutely correct," she said tartly.

"Well then, I made the right decision, didn't I?" he said with a fake smile.

She narrowed her eyes at him. "Why are you here? Do you have more bad news that you had to tell me in person?"

He ignored her barbed question and walked over to where she stood. She tightened the towel around her torso.

"Who was that man you were with two nights ago, at happy hour after work?"

"You were following me?" she said with wide eyes.

"Not me personally."

"But you had someone do it?"

"Yes," Andres answered in a clipped tone.

"You had no right." She put distance between them by walking closer to the bed.

"Maybe I got a little jealous."

"Jealous?" Angela laughed softly. "Aren't you supposed to be going through a list of women to choose a wife?"

"Do you intend to throw that in my face every time we speak to each other?"

"I really had no intention of ever speaking to you again, to be quite honest. What with you having to get married and all."

"This isn't the way that I wanted things to go, you know that. I wanted to continue seeing you, but you chose to end it." He wished he could hold or touch her, but her anger kept him at bay.

"Why would I continue to see you when you told me you have to get married? I'm not interested in your little arrangement, so you can go to hell, Andres."

"Only if you come with me," he grated.

She glared at him. "What do you want? We're over. We're done."

"I had to see you." His jaw clenched as he fought back intense emotion. "To stop you from…from…"

"From what? From moving on with my life after you dumped me?"

He didn't know what he'd expected when he showed up here, but this conversation was not going well at all. "Are you seeing that man?"

"No."

"Then who is he?"

"None of your business."

"On the contrary, everything about you is my business."

She laughed again. "Since when?"

"Since I can't get you out of my mind. Since I called and you didn't answer." His eyes bored into hers and tension made his body rigid.

"I will never answer another phone call from you. He's my co-worker. We went for drinks. That's it. Satisfied?"

He almost sagged in relief.

"You shouldn't be here."

"I know." He sank onto the bed and bent his head, his hands curling into fists on his thighs, all of the fight drained from him. "I know, and yet here I am. Because I miss you."

"It's only been a couple of weeks," she said in a low voice.

"It's been an eternity."

"Don't do this," she said in a trembling voice.

His hand encircled her slender wrist and tugged her forward, his way of signaling that she should straddle him, but she curled her fingers into a fist and stood firm.

"You miss me, too," he said.

"Of course I do. I can't turn off my feelings like a faucet."

He wanted her close. He tugged again, and this time she reluctantly came to stand between his legs. He kissed her belly through the towel. She didn't pull away from him, and he saw that as a good sign. Bolder, he pulled on the towel and let it fall to the floor.

His hungry gaze swept over her feminine form. Over her breasts capped by caramel-colored nipples, her tawny-gold skin, and down to the strip of hair between her hips.

Gently, he lowered her onto the bed. He kissed her bare shoulder and dragged his tongue along the dip in her collarbone. She smelled and tasted so good, he wanted to swallow her whole.

His mouth found hers and indulged in the softness and sweetness of her lips. This wasn't why he'd come, but his body was hard, and his erection strained against his pants.

She whimpered and cupped the back of his head, kissing him

back wholeheartedly, making him believe for a split second that he could have heaven again. Then she froze. Her kisses stopped and her hand fell away. Andres lifted his head and saw that sadness filled her eyes.

"Don't do this to me again. We already said goodbye."

"Angela…" He dropped his head to her shoulder. "You know I had no choice."

"Yes, I do. So why are you here?" she asked in a thick voice. "Nothing is going to change. Go back to Europe and marry your princess or whatever you're supposed to do. Leave me alone. Stop hurting me."

He felt her hurt like his own. He hurt, too.

"What you're doing isn't fair. It's selfish. Love isn't selfish," Angela said.

She couldn't have hurt him more if she'd driven a stake through his heart.

Andres lifted up from the bed. "You're right." He always got what he wanted, and he was determined to hold onto her, though he knew he shouldn't. That wasn't fair to her. His behavior was reprehensible. "I won't bother you again."

Andres didn't look back. He went down the stairs and out the back the way he'd come. He trudged through the grass and walked the couple of blocks to the waiting sedan.

Ollie, leaning against the vehicle, straightened when he saw Andres. "Your Highness…?"

Andres didn't make eye contact. "We're going home," he said.

He let himself into the car and shut the door.

23

Angela sat outside her parents' home, dreading the conversation she needed to have with them. Finally, she worked up the nerve and exited the car. She walked in a daze up the driveway. Per usual, Rebecca's red sedan was parked there, but she hoped her sister wasn't around. She needed privacy to speak to her parents.

She still couldn't believe what she'd learned today. She'd taken the day off to run some errands, one of which was to go to the doctor. A couple of days ago she could no longer ignore the fact that she hadn't had a period in a while. She'd taken three pregnancy tests, all of them positive, and still she'd been in denial.

Until today.

Today she learned that she was pregnant and had no clue what to do.

It was strange to think of herself as pregnant because she hadn't noticed any changes in her body. None of the ones that she typically heard about, anyway. She rested a hand on her stomach in amazement. No morning sickness, no cravings, no tiredness, and no tender breasts. Yet she was definitely pregnant.

She entered the house and her mother came toward her with her arms outstretched.

"Hello, baby," she said.

"Hi, Mom." Angela squeezed her mother back. "Where's Becky?"

"Upstairs asleep." Her mother kept her voice neutral, but Angela knew that she was not pleased Rebecca was still there.

"Where's Dad?"

"In the den watching TV. I was upstairs when I saw your car pull up."

They entered the den, and sure enough her father, Martin, sat in his recliner with his legs up, watching the news. His hand rested on the remote on the arm of the chair, and he wore glasses perched on his nose.

"Hey, there. Is that my baby?" he asked with a wide grin.

"Yes, it's me." Angela bent down and kissed his ruddy cheek. She ran a hand over his silky brown hair. "You have a few more gray strands," she teased.

He chuckled. "When men get gray hair it makes them look distinguished, don't you know."

"That's so unfair," her mother said. Tessa sat down on the sofa next to her husband's chair.

Martin shrugged. "I don't make the rules."

"What brings you by? Not that we're not happy to see you, but we know how busy you are with your job and everything, and you're here in the middle of the week during work hours." Tessa crossed her legs.

Angela took a deep breath. "I have something to tell you. Dad, do you mind turning off the TV?"

Her parents glanced quickly at each other, but her father did as she requested.

"What is it, dear?" Concern filled her mother's dark eyes.

Too antsy to sit, Angela stood in front of the coffee table and faced both of her parents. "There is no other way to say this except to say it bluntly. I'm pregnant."

Stunned silence filled the room. Both of her parents stared at her.

"Nothing to say?" she asked carefully.

Tessa blinked, looked at her husband, and then looked at Angela. "Well, I'm not sure how to react. Is this something that you're happy about?"

"I–I'm not sure. Part of me is excited and another part of me feels overwhelmed. I never thought that I would be a single mother, and I certainly didn't plan to have a baby. I found out today, and I'm still digesting the idea of being pregnant."

She touched a hand to her stomach and her father's gaze followed the movement. He pushed down the foot rest on the recliner, sat up straight, and leaned forward.

"I didn't know you were dating anyone seriously. Who's the father?"

Angela licked her lips and glanced at her mother. "You're not going to believe me when I tell you."

She told them the whole story of how she had met Andres in Zamibia and the fact that they had carried on a secret relationship after he came to the States to do business with her company.

"Well, that was certainly unexpected," Martin said. "A prince? An *actual* prince? How did you manage to keep this a secret?"

"Through careful planning," Angela replied.

"And what does he say? Or have you not told him yet?" her mother asked.

"I haven't told him yet," Angela admitted.

"But you do plan to tell him, don't you?"

"At some point." Angela ambled over to a corner cabinet that held the awards in business and music her father had accrued over the years.

"But...?" Tessa prompted.

Angela faced her parents and folded her arms over her abdomen. "But I don't know how and I don't know when. Against my better judgment, I looked him up recently and the announcement has been made. Andres will be the new ruler of Estoria, and not only that, he's already started..." Her voice faltered. "Started the selection process for a wife. Rumor has it that he went to see a member of the royal family in Spain."

She swallowed down the pain in her chest. She should have never gone online to search for news about him, but in a moment of weakness she looked into what he was doing.

Tessa came toward her and put an arm around her shoulders. "If you don't tell him you're pregnant, you're not in this alone. Your father and I will be there for you."

"Wait a minute now. We are going to be there for her, but she *has* to tell him about the child." Her father's voice was firm.

"I do plan to tell him, I just…"

Her mother's arms tightened around her. "You don't have to rush into anything. You still have time. How far along are you?"

"Nine weeks."

Her mother rubbed her back, which helped Angela relax.

"You have plenty of time."

"He has a right to know, Angela," her father said.

"I know."

"He may want to be a part of that child's life, even if he's married to someone else."

Angela nodded numbly.

"That's enough talk about this," her mother said. "I have pound cake and coffee. Let's get some of that and relax and think about the positive. I'm going to be a grandmother, you're going to be a grandfather. We'll deal with the rest later. Agreed?" She looked from one to the other.

Angela nodded to appease her. "Agreed."

"Good. I'll be right back." Tessa disappeared from the room.

Martin patted the area her mother had vacated, and Angela walked slowly to the sofa and sat down.

"Whatever decision you make, you know your mom and I will be there for you. You're my baby." He took her hand in his.

Having two supporting parents was a godsend, and frankly, she'd been able to count on them all her life. It was comforting to know that wouldn't change now.

"A twenty-nine-year-old baby," she said, with amusement in her voice.

"And don't you forget it." Martin chuckled and squeezed her hand. "I want to make sure you're okay. Are you?"

"I will be. Thank you," Angela whispered.

24

Angela walked from the parking lot toward the front of the Myers-Gomez building. Work was even more of a chore nowadays. Everything she did was now a chore that she didn't look forward to. She wished the day was already over.

Her footsteps slowed when she saw a bunch of people standing outside. Some carried microphones, and others held video cameras.

What in the world was going on?

Frowning, she walked slowly toward the group with the intention of going around them.

Then someone yelled, "There she is!"

All of a sudden, the reporters swarmed toward her like a group of geese, pushing microphones into her face and yelling questions. Angela flinched and pushed her hands up to ward them off.

"Is it true that you're the secret lover of Prince Andres of Estoria?"

"Is it true that you're pregnant with his baby?"

What?

Startled, Angela froze before she caught herself and made an effort to bolt through the crowd with her head bowed low. The group didn't let her pass and crowded more tightly around her. She was locked in, scarcely able to move. She elbowed through them with her head ducked as questions came at her from the right, left, front, and back.

"No comment! No comment!" she screamed.

She kept moving, unable to take more than small steps that kept her progress painfully slow.

Closer to the building, she heard a voice yell, "Let her in!"

She looked up and saw Carl, the security guard, coming through the door. "Let her in!" he yelled again.

His burly body plowed through them, and he shoved a particularly aggressive woman out of his way and yanked Angela into the atrium by the wrist. He threw an arm around her shoulders and used his towering frame as a shield, escorting her to the bank of elevators out of the view of the reporters and curious onlookers who openly held up phones to videotape the ruckus.

"What the hell was that?" Angela asked, her voice shaking.

Carl's gaze was sympathetic. "They're all here for you. They've been here since I arrived this morning and tried to get in, but we kept them out. If I'd known your number, I would've called to warn you."

"Thank you," Angela replied. She was shaking, but at least she was safely inside the building.

The security guard nodded and left her to return to the front of the building.

Instead of taking the elevator to her office on the tenth floor, Angela took the elevator to the fifth floor instead. She stepped off and with a quick glance found the public restroom.

She went in and saw that it was empty. She stared at her face in the mirror. Her eyes looked particularly wild, and heightened color tainted her cheeks.

Panic seized her, and she remembered another time when she'd been hounded by the press. She suddenly felt faint, so overcome she started hyperventilating. She dropped her messenger bag and purse to the floor and, clutching her tight chest, staggered into the end stall and dropped onto the seat. She placed her head between her knees and breathed deeply to keep from passing out.

They knew. Angela squeezed her eyes shut.

Somehow, these people knew about Andres and the baby. But how? The only person she'd told was her parents. She hadn't even told Dahlia yet.

Eventually, she calmed enough to take slow, cleansing breaths. She lifted her head. She had to find a way to function for the rest of the day, for the sake of her job and that of her clients.

Angela picked up her belongings and took the elevator up to her floor.

"Good morning," she said to the male receptionist when she stepped off.

"Good morning." Was it her imagination, or did he look at her funny? How many of her co-workers knew what was going on?

Slowly, she made her way to her office and shut the door. After about fifteen minutes of trying to work, she had to stop. Her head throbbed, and though she hated taking painkillers, she'd have to today because she suspected this headache wasn't going away anytime soon.

She decided to make a cup of tea. It wasn't her usual beverage of choice, but the thought of a steaming cup of Earl Grey was suddenly very appealing.

She went to the door and opened it but stopped short when she saw her boss standing on the other side, his hand raised as if he were about to knock.

"Edgar."

"Can we talk for a minute?" he asked.

"Sure. Of course." Angela smoothed her hands down her skirt and led the way back into the office. She stood beside her desk and waited. "How can I help you?"

He pursed his lips. "I normally don't care what happens in the private lives of my employees," he began. "But there seems to be commotion around your personal life. Care to talk about it?"

She took a deep breath and exhaled silently. "I suppose you're talking about the reporters downstairs?"

"What do you think?"

"I don't know why they're here. I'm not involved in anything newsworthy."

"You're not dating a European prince, a former client, from Estoria?" He arched a brow.

Her shoulders dropped in defeat. "I was, but not anymore. There's really no reason for them to be outside."

"So the fact that you're pregnant with his child is irrelevant?"

Dammit. Angela briefly closed her eyes. "I'm really sorry about this, Edgar."

"Maybe you need a break from work for a while—"

"No!" Without work, she didn't have anything except plenty of time to think about Andres. "I'll get this sorted out, I promise."

Edgar tucked a hand into his pants pocket. "This is not a good situation, Angela. You're one of my best consultants, so you do understand that we run a business here, a very profitable business with clients who won't look too kindly on this type of…sensationalism around our company. Reporters with cameras and microphones lurking around the door is not a good look."

"I understand, but I promise you, this problem will go away very soon." She didn't know why she said that. She had no proof that would be the case. "And to put your mind at ease, I assure you, what happened downstairs will not affect my work."

"I'm not concerned about your work. I'm concerned about the negative press that will result, which could affect our company," Edgar said in a grave tone. "First thing in the morning, these reporters have already been very disruptive. You know as well as I do that some of our clients value their anonymity, and we could lose business if our clients—and future clients—see the kind of nonsense I saw out there this morning. And staff…" He huffed.

"They shouldn't have to fight that mob to get to work. You under-stand that, don't you?"

"Yes, I do," Angela said quietly.

"Good. Then handle it. If you don't, I have to give you time off to get your affairs in order. Because we can't allow this to continue, are we clear?"

"Yes, we're clear."

25

This was a nightmare. It had to be nightmare.

Angela took a deep breath as she faced her reflection in the bathroom mirror at work.

In a few short days, both her personal life and work life had fallen apart. One embarrassing headline proclaimed that she was set for the next eighteen years, as if she'd gotten pregnant on purpose. Some employees, including her good buddy Livia, became standoffish. They seemed uncomfortable with her newfound notoriety and the effect it had on the firm. Others hovered around, coyly asking questions to get more information about her fling with a royal. When she refused to give them any information, they eventually went back to their desks.

Then, a few days ago, she'd been taken off a major project at the request of one of the clients and was fairly certain she would be removed from others. As if things couldn't get any worse, the details about her past relationship with pop artist Liam resurfaced, and now she was seen as an upwardly mobile femme fatale who sank her claws into unsuspecting rich men to milk them of their money. How ironic, considering she prided herself on her independence.

She didn't know for sure who the "source" in the articles was but suspected it was her sister. Seeing the words "obnoxious," "arrogant," and "hoity-toity" in the news—words Rebecca had used to refer to her in the past—made her think that. Rebecca would do anything for money, and Angela suspected that she must have overhead the conversation with her parents and sold the news to the tabloids. She'd since disappeared, but Angela was certain she'd be back when the money ran out.

Angela had taken to wearing disguises and donned oversized sunglasses and a blonde wig as she prepared to leave work for the day. These extreme measures were, unfortunately, necessary. She arrived at work much earlier and left later nowadays, in disguise, to avoid the reporters, but she wouldn't be surprised if they caught on to her trick. She ordered in lunch or had a co-worker bring her a sandwich when they returned from their own meal. She was practically trapped in the Myers-Gomez building because the media hounds wouldn't go away.

"You got this," she said to her reflection.

She rolled her neck and exited the bathroom with her messenger bag over one shoulder, and her purse and car keys in hand. She dreaded the trip home because she didn't have a home anymore. She couldn't go to her parents' because the press hounded them there, and for the past few days she'd been renting a one-bedroom apartment, thanks to Airbnb. She'd temporarily abandoned her house after the press discovered where she lived. Mr. Jefferson had called one night to check on her, and after confirming she was all right, she hung up before she burst into tears.

A wave of apprehension tightened her body as the elevator landed on the first floor. She was going out the back as another precautionary measure. She wondered how much longer she'd have to put up with the reporters until they lost interest and moved on to the next hot topic.

Cold air hit her face when she exited the building. Her stride faltered and she tensed when movement to the right caught her eye. To her dismay, she recognized one of the reporters walking briskly toward her.

"I just want to talk," he said. He'd obviously been waiting out there for a while and needed to keep warm, so like her, he was buttoned up in a coat and wore a scarf around his neck.

"No comment," Angela said firmly, but her voice trembled. Why didn't they leave her alone?

Another reporter approached from her left and a photographer stepped out of his car and started snapping pictures. They'd figured out her plan. Tears filled Angela's eyes as panic beat into her chest.

"Just a word, Ms. Lipscomb," the female reporter called out. Blonde hair streamed behind her as she rushed toward Angela.

"Go away! Leave me alone!" Angela screamed.

She hurried down the stairs, but in her haste missed her footing. She twisted her ankle on the bottom step and stumbled, arms flailing as she tried to regain her balance. At the last moment, before she sprawled across the pavement, two strong hands grabbed her and held her upright.

"Get back!" said a firm male voice with a Spanish accent.

Andres!

Angela looked up into his grim face and gripped his arm.

He wasn't looking at her. He glowered at the people who had been trying to accost her. As she watched, Ollie and three other bodyguards created a barrier between them and the media hawks.

Andres hustled her away.

"Prince Andres, wait! Do you have a comment about your relationship with Miss Lipscomb?"

"I only have a few questions! Your Highness!"

He guided her to a limo about a hundred feet away, which she hadn't noticed before because it had been out of her line of sight when she exited the building.

She glanced back and saw that the four guards remained in position as human shields and didn't allow any of the media to follow her and Andres.

She kept up with Andres's brisk steps as best she could, and when they arrived at the car he swung open the door and they piled in. He pulled her into his arms and she slumped against him.

"Are you hurt?" he asked anxiously. He grasped her shoulders.

Angela shook her head. She couldn't utter a word. She was relieved but still terrified. Her lips trembled.

"Angela," he said in a harder tone. "Are you hurt?" He removed the sunglasses and looked into her eyes as if searching for the truth.

"No," she said in a weak voice.

She felt utterly helpless in that moment, and when he pulled her into his arms and squeezed her tight, she held on just as tight, taking strength from him.

"You're safe now." He rubbed her back, soothing her trembling body against his. "Go. Now!" he barked at Gustave.

They pulled away from the curb and Angela closed her eyes. She had no idea where they were going but knew Andres would take care of everything.

ANDRES LEFT the cockpit after giving the pilots new instructions. He'd told Angela he wanted to take her away from Atlanta, and she hadn't put up a fight.

He entered the living room in time to see her take a cup of warm tea from the flight attendant with a soft "Thank you."

The past week had clearly taken a toll. She looked exhausted. He would have come sooner if he'd known, but he'd stopped keeping tabs on her when she requested he leave her alone. He only found out what was happening because the story about her being pregnant with his baby had reached Europe and the ears of the palace PR team.

She had removed the wig and wore her long, dark hair smoothed over one shoulder. After a warm shower, the flight attendant had given her toiletries and the comfy cotton pants and long-sleeve shirt she now wore. She sat with her legs curled up on the sofa, waiting for Andres's appearance.

Hands in his pockets, he halted in the middle of the floor. "Is it mine?" he asked, though he already knew the answer. He simply needed to get confirmation from her.

She didn't bother to pretend to not know what he was talking about. "Yes."

"Were you going to tell me?"

"Yes, but I didn't get a chance to." She sipped the tea and then leaned forward to set it on the table in front of her. "Where are we going?

Andres sat down on the sofa across from her and spread his arms across the back. "To Estoria," he said calmly.

Angela stared him with a deep frown that made it clear she thought she misunderstood. "What did you say?"

"You heard me."

"Why? I thought we were going back to Florida, or—or some other state to get away and figure out what to do. You can't take me out of the country!" She jumped up and went to one of the windows. She peered out into the night sky, as if she could tell the direction of the plane by sight alone.

There was a moment of silence as he waited. She rounded on him. "You tricked me. You pretended to rescue me but you've kidnapped me for a transatlantic flight to Estoria. I don't even know you. You're a monster!"

"Yes, I'm a monster. A monster who refuses to be apart from his child. Did you really think I would allow any child of mine to live in a world apart from me, feeling unloved by his or her own father? *Never*." He'd suffered that pain. He would not inflict it on his own child. "If that makes me a monster, then so be it, but you are coming to Estoria with me."

"This isn't how you handle a difficult situation. Think about what you're saying. You can't do this."

"It has already been done."

"What about me? This isn't what I want."

"What you or I want is no longer the only concern in our individual lives. We have to think of our child, and I have to think about the future of my country. My plan was to take you to Miami or someplace else close by. But after our conversation, I decided this would be best."

"*You* decided, and what about my things? My belongings."

"All will be handled from Estoria. You will also be able to resign from your position at Myers-Gomez."

"You thought of everything."

"Of course." He stood. "You're carrying my child, Angela. Did you really think that I would simply walk away?"

"Not walk away, but I thought you came to talk. We need to discuss what's going to happen in detail. Discuss arrangements for how we'll handle this pregnancy and co-parenting."

His blue gaze dropped to her midsection before finding hers again. "Discuss? There is no discussion to be had. You know I need an heir." A thread of anger laced his words.

"You need a wife. That's what you told me. A child born outside of marriage can't be in line for the throne." She blushed. She obviously hadn't meant to divulge that she'd researched the possibility of her child becoming next in line for the throne.

"That is correct, if the child is born outside of marriage. But our child won't be. You and I are getting married."

She gaped at him and then burst into laughter. "You can't be serious. I'm not interested. I have a job. I have a home. I have family back in Georgia. I can't up and leave all of that behind. I will not be marrying you simply because I'm pregnant."

"Then you will stay with me until you change your mind. There is only one answer for you to give me, and that answer is yes."

"I can't."

"You don't have a choice."

"I do have a choice!" Her voice elevated. She pressed a hand to her chest and took a calming breath. Speaking in a quieter voice, she said, "I planned to tell you about the pregnancy because it was the right thing to do, but you know now. What more do you want from me?"

"If you marry me, everything will fall into place."

"Everything? What are you talking about? You're in the middle of searching for a wife. Once you're married, you'll have plenty of babies with your new bride."

"I've called off the search."

"You have? Why?"

Andres slowly rolled up the cuffs on his sleeves. "Because as I told you, I'm going to marry you instead." He hit a button on a panel in the wall and his assistant's voice came through the speaker. "Yes, Your Highness."

Angela sank into the chair. She wasn't looking at him.

"Have the housekeepers prepare The Cream Room in my apartment for Miss Lipscomb."

"Yes, sir."

Andres hung up, and Angela lifted doleful eyes to his. "Before you left Estoria, did you ask your grandfather for approval to marry me?"

She was no fool. She was a smart woman with a sharp mind. Wasn't that one of the reasons he loved her? Prince Felipe had not supported the marriage and told Andres so in very clear, succinct words.

Andres didn't answer the question directly. "I will handle my grandfather."

A sad smile crossed her lips. "This isn't going to work."

Andres swallowed down his concern. He hoped she was wrong.

26

"Have you lost your mind?" Felipe bellowed. His eyes flashed with a fire Andres hadn't seen in years.

"I am perfectly sane," Andres replied calmly.

With renewed vigor, Felipe marched across the floor of his office to get in Andres's face.

His body stiffened, but he remained firmly in place, willing and ready to face the consequences of his actions.

"Bringing her here to marry her goes against everything I told you to do."

"She's pregnant."

"And what of it? Kings and princes have been getting women pregnant since the beginning of time. That doesn't mean you have to marry her. Look at Prince Albert of Monaco."

"I am not Prince Albert!" Andres shot back.

Felipe ran wrinkled fingers across his well-coiffed hair. "This is unlike you, Andres. This woman has fried your brain. You clearly haven't thought through what you have done."

"I have thought it through, and marrying Angela is the best decision."

Granted, bringing her to Estoria had been a spur-of-the-moment decision. When he'd picked her up at her place of employment, he'd simply gone there to find her and speak to her. After keeping watch on the building the day before, Ollie, with his eagle eyes, had let him know that she left through the back in disguise.

But once he'd seen how shaken up she'd been, and knowing that she carried his child, he'd made the impromptu decision to bring her here where she'd be safe. And if he were honest, bring her here to show her what she was missing so he could convince her to marry him.

How was he supposed to go on with his life and share a bed with another woman when the woman he really wanted and loved was over four thousand miles away? Yes, his actions had been drastic, but nothing else mattered. Not tradition. Not his grandfather's request. He wanted Angela and his unborn child.

"And what about the Swedes or the Spanish? You've already expressed interest in choosing a bride from among them," his grandfather said.

"I will handle them."

"We should form an alliance with another country that benefits us. What does this woman have to offer our country?"

"An heir to the throne," Andres answered between gritted teeth.

"You do not have a legitimate heir unless you marry, and I will not give my approval." Felipe's face settled into harsh, angry lines. "We don't have much time. The announcement has been made. You must take the throne in less than a year, and you must be married. This woman has bewitched you. Let her have the child but marry someone else."

"I will marry her," Andres insisted.

"Even if I give my approval, which I won't. You should consider her feelings, and not only your own. You would expose her to the barbs and hurtful words of people who don't accept her? To people who will be angry about you marrying a goddamn commoner and an American?"

"We could lead our country into a new era, with new ideas and traditions. *We* lead, and our countrymen follow our example. Are you telling me there is no room for change?"

"I am telling you that you are a fool and will regret what you have done."

"Then let me be a fool. I stand firm in my decision. How many more people should suffer for the sake of tradition, Grandfather? Should I live the rest of my life in misery like my father? Should I marry someone I don't love, the way you had to?"

Felipe flinched, but instead of coming back at him after the harsh words he spoke, his grandfather's face slowly transformed into one of shock. "You really are a damn fool. You've made the same mistake I did. You've fallen in love with her." He shook his head and suddenly looked very tired. "I cannot give my blessing. Not when I know you're wrong."

"You have to change your mind."

"I cannot. There is very little room for change in our world. Mark my words. You *will* regret this."

THREE DAYS. For three days Angela had been forced to remain in this room without access to a phone. She paced the floor restlessly. She didn't know what to do with herself.

Two men guarded the door outside, and like a prisoner, she'd been allowed only one phone call when she arrived. She'd called her parents, told them where she was, and assured them she was well. Not because she wanted to protect Andres, but because she didn't want them to worry.

After all, she was well. The walk-in closet was not completely filled but contained an array of outfits for her to choose from. She wore one of the outfits now, a sleeveless, knee-length floral print dress with flower-shaped buttons down the bodice.

Though she was a prisoner, the room Andres chose for her was lovely, decorated in creams and earth tones and looking out onto the water. Blue ocean sparkled in the distance below rolling green hills run through with cobble-stoned streets and dotted with houses and commercial buildings. From the palace, she had a good view, and much of the country seemed to live along the coasts, which was where the majority of the buildings were concentrated. The eastern coast was untouched, where Andres anticipated building an eco-friendly tourist attraction to diversify the nation's revenue stream.

Her meals were all served in here and were absolutely delicious. Andres ate with her last night and gave her an update. Apparently, a member of his staff, pretending to be her, had requested a leave of absence from Edgar, and the news agencies had received an anonymous tip with the same information. She glared at him across the table when he told her that, but no doubt Edgar was pleased to have peace and calm return to the company.

She demanded that Andres apologize and let her go back home, but they were both stubborn. He refused to apologize so she refused to speak to him. She gave him the silent treatment throughout the entire meal until he finally grumbled something in Spanish and left.

A knock sounded on the door.

Angela turned away from the window. "Come in."

Andres entered. He looked exhausted but held his head at the same regal tilt, as if he'd done nothing wrong. "Are you comfortable?" he asked.

"As comfortable as a prisoner could be."

"Don't say that."

"Then be reasonable. You have guards outside the door. I can't use the phone. You took my computer. My only contact with the outside world is the television—where everything is in Spanish—and when staff comes in to check on me or bring food. I haven't been outside in days. You can't keep me here forever, and you can't force me to marry you."

"This is only temporary."

"How long is temporary?"

He frowned. "Are you telling me that none of this appeals to you? Marrying me and building a life together? You told me you loved me."

"And you said you loved me. Is this how you treat someone you love?"

"What do you want me to do? Let you walk out of my life and take my child with you? I cannot do that. I cannot let you go. So we will figure out a way to make this work."

"And why isn't it working? What's the problem, Andres?"

His lips tightened.

"Your grandfather," Angela guessed.

"Give me time. I can convince him."

"You can convince him? I'm a commoner. I don't have a title or rank, and you told me yourself that tradition requires you marry a woman descended from nobility. What will your family say? What will your people say? Do you really think they'll accept me?"

"They will have no choice if we marry."

"Oh, so we'll just shove it down their throats. Good idea. And the fact that I never wanted to be famous doesn't matter to you."

"Of course it matters to me." His eyes softened and he came toward her. He caught her chin. "I'm sorry you had to go through that, but everyone knows about us now. It will get easier, I promise. We'll make sure you have the best media training available. You can gradually move into your role as a princess, take time to learn your duties. I only need you to be patient and give me time to convince my grandfather. Once he approves our marriage, everything will change. You'll see."

"And what about me? The problem isn't just that I'm a commoner." She held her hand up to his eye level. "It's time we address the elephant in the room. I'm half Black, Andres."

"That doesn't matter to me."

"Does it matter to him?"

"No. I'm certain of it." He took her hand and kissed the inside of her wrist. "I can't be without you. I tried, and I was miserable.

Stay with me. Make a life with me. You have nothing to fear. I will protect you. Trust me, this will work."

He backed up to the bed and sat on the edge of the mattress. He gently tugged on her hand, and she placed a knee on either side of his thighs. Looking down into his eyes, she saw his sincerity.

"What if you're wrong?"

"I'm not."

"You promise? You promise we'll be okay?" she asked.

Her voice trembled with emotion and fear of the unknown. She would have to give up everything she knew to learn a new culture, customs, and protocol. But with him by her side, she might have the strength to suffer through whatever came her way.

"I promise," he whispered. "Tell me you're no longer angry at me."

"One minute you're dumping me to go through a list of potential brides, the next you're kidnapping me. I'm still angry at you." She thumped him on the shoulder, and he winced. "But...not as angry as I was two days ago."

"So you'll give me time?"

She traced his mouth with her thumb. "Yes, I guess."

His face broke into a wide grin.

"Get that smile off your face!"

Andres chuckled and kissed her neck and squeezed her tight. He fisted his hands into her hair. "I love you, Angela Lipscomb. Will you marry me?"

She gazed into his eyes. While she hadn't forgotten the pain of his betrayal, she believed in his love. She nodded. "Yes."

Andres let out a breath of relief and kissed her hard. She realized that even in his confidence, he'd still had doubts.

He slid his hands down her back and massaged her ass through the thin fabric of her dress.

Angela let out a little moan. "Andres, this is the last thing we should be doing."

"Why?" He sucked on the fleshy, lower part of her ear.

Angela moaned again and tilted her head back. "Because it's the middle of the day and you have work to do."

"I can do my work later. I haven't made love to you in so long." His husky voice in her ear made the pulse in her neck thrum faster.

"Andres," she whispered. The sweet ache of desire filled the space between her legs.

Her rolled her onto her back and pressed a kiss to her stomach. "I can't wait until you start showing."

"Me either," Angela admitted. She smiled, while biting into her bottom lip.

Andres palmed her flat stomach and then dropped another kiss dead center on her belly. "I can't wait to meet you," he said in a low voice.

His voice was so tender and filled with emotion, tears pricked her eyes.

He glanced up at her. "I need you, *amor*. *Ahora*."

Andres kissed lower on her body and pushed the hem of the dress higher. Then he dragged his tongue along the inside of her legs and tugged her panties down past her knees before tossing them to the floor.

The buttons at the top of her dress were forced apart with an impatient yank. Lust tightened her exposed nipples. He fastened his mouth over one caramel-tipped breast and she arched into the titillating tug of his lips.

He released her nipple and kissed up the column of her neck. "You're mine again," he whispered.

"Yes," she whispered back.

He devoured her lips as he undid his pants. Her bare feet shoved the pants and his underwear past his hips, and he bore down on her with the force of a runaway train. When their bodies connected, they both sucked in deep breaths.

She'd missed him so much. Angela clamped her legs around him and pushed her hands under his shirt. She explored his sides and caressed the muscles in his back—anywhere her hands could reach.

"You're mine," Andres growled.

Her head tilted back as she gave herself over to the unbearable, exquisite pleasure of his possession. Their bodies moved in sync, with every thrust taking her higher until she cried out in a shivering climax.

27

W ith the phone pressed to her ear, Angela said, "Leave my godson alone."

She was talking to Dahlia, who'd just scolded her son, Noel.

"Do you want him? Because I think he's figured out he's a prince and is starting to get out of control."

Angela giggled. "Or he's a typical toddler," she said.

"That, too," Dahlia admitted.

Angela leisurely lifted a foot out of the warm, scented water of her bath. She'd turn into a prune if she stayed in there too much longer, but this was the perfect end to what had been a hectic week.

"How are things going?" Dahlia asked.

"Better, but at times it's *a lot*."

Andres had relaxed his restrictions, so she had a phone now. And while she thought she might be bored without the challenges of a career to occupy her time, she quickly learned there were other challenges that awaited her if she were to marry him. She would join him in managing The Crown's income-generating properties and their business interests here and abroad. As the country's top diplomats, they would travel to other countries to build relationships and act as hosts when top-ranking dignitaries came to their shores. She would also join Andres on various charitable boards, and while his main projects involved the environment, she was expected to find a cause of her own to champion.

There were quite a few "rules" she'd have to follow, too. She could no longer use a cell phone in public nor was she allowed to complain about being sick. She'd simply have to suck it up until she was able to privately speak to her aides or one of the palace physicians. She had to learn Spanish, so two days ago a tutor arrived to schedule her lessons, along with an etiquette coach to get her up to speed on royal protocol.

She and Andres went horseback riding so he could show her the land and took a helicopter ride to the eastern end of the island where they witnessed otters frolicking in the waves. She went to the palace library several hours a day to read about the history of the country and walked the grounds to not only stretch her legs but learn her way around. One day while Andres was tied up in meetings, she went on a short trip into the capital city and visited the harbor where the cargo ships and ferries came in from the mainland.

"I understand the 'it's a lot' part. I was scared, terrified, at how much I had to learn and worried that I'd screw up, embarrass myself and cause irreparable harm to the royal family." Dahlia laughed softly. "It's not easy being under this type of scrutiny, but my advice is to not stress too much, and lean on Andres. He's lived in this world his entire life.

"I have a full staff to support me, but more than anything, learning the ropes is made easier because of Kofi. Not only does he understand this life, but he works hard to make sure that I fit in and understand my role. If you don't have that with Andres, it's going to make fitting in harder. You have to know that he's supportive of you, and you have to be a team or the relationship won't work. Yes, you have access to vast amounts of wealth and power, but that life is also very isolating because you can't come and go as you please, and you have to adhere to royal protocol and other rules and regulations that will blow your mind. But if you and Andres are in this together, the way that Kofi and I are, then it will be so much easier. And it could potentially strengthen your love."

"Thanks, I needed that. I do have Andres's support, which is wonderful. But in our case, it might not be enough. I wish I knew what his grandfather was thinking. What if I go through all of this training and he still doesn't approve of us getting married?"

"You haven't met him yet?"

"No," Angela replied glumly.

During all this time, she had expected to be summoned to meet Prince Felipe but hadn't been. She remained patient but anxious. Did his grandfather not want to meet her at all, or was he just busy? Andres wouldn't say, and she hid her concern from him. If his grandfather, the man he most admired in the world, didn't sign off on their wedding, then it wouldn't happen.

Angela settled lower in the tub, letting her head rest against the waterproof pillow behind her. "I'm worried," she admitted. "I'm afraid he'll never agree to us getting married, and then what?"

"Aren't they supposed to be the rebel kingdom of Europe?"

"They're not that rebellious," Angela said dryly. "And I get the impression Prince Felipe is staunchly conservative and believes in following custom."

Dahlia paused for several seconds before replying. "How much have you been exposed to the media while you're there?"

"What do you mean?"

"Do you have access to newspapers and magazines? Have you seen the news?"

Angela thought for a minute. "Now that you mention it, I haven't seen any papers since I've been here. I've been so busy I haven't paid much attention to the news, and everything is in Spanish anyway, so I have no idea what they're saying. Why?"

Dahlia fell silent again.

A knot of dread settled in the pit of Angela's stomach. "Hey, you're making me nervous," she said with a little laugh. "Is there something I should know?"

"I don't want to cause you to worry, but yes, there is something you should know."

"Is it my sister again? Andres sent people to talk to her and my parents."

Andres had sent several aides to look into the leak about her pregnancy and the disparaging remarks made about Angela. They discovered that her sister had indeed been the "source." The visit with her parents was to get them ready for the wedding to come and the interest their marriage would generate in the general public. The conversation with Rebecca was to see how to put a stop to her making any more remarks about Angela to the press. A large amount of money and an ironclad NDA that threatened her with harsh legal consequences had been used to shut down her sister. Sad that her own sister hadn't been thoughtful enough to keep quiet on her own.

"Listen, I'm going to send you some English-language newspapers and magazines. We're best friends, and you should know what's being said about you," Dahlia said quietly.

"It's bad, isn't it?"

"Yes, but remember what I said. You and Andres are a team. Lean on him and you'll work through it together."

"If we were a team, he would have told me what you're telling me now."

"He's probably trying to protect you."

Angela sighed. "Yeah." He'd said he would protect her, but if protecting her meant keeping her in the dark about what was happening around her, she didn't want that kind of protection. "How soon can you send me the papers?"

"Give me a few days."

"Thanks."

FOUR HUNDRED YEARS AGO, European powers took Miss Lipscomb's ancestors from the shores of the dark continent as human cargo. Today, she's carrying the most valuable cargo there is—the heir to the throne of a European principality. How times have changed!

WE EXPECTED a political alliance with a Swedish noblewoman or a Spanish princess. Instead, we have an American with an exotic bloodline.

IS Prince Andres now a baby daddy? While the palace refuses to confirm or deny the rumors that Miss Lipscomb is pregnant, sources tell us…

AS THE FIRST non-white person to marry into the House of Vasquez, Miss Lipscomb has made quite the catch. Less than one hundred years ago, she would have been Prince Andres's bed wench. Today, she is about to marry into one of Europe's oldest monarchies.

¡MIERDA! Andres tossed another newspaper onto his desk with an angry growl. "What the hell is going on in this country?" he demanded of his secretary, Ronaldo.

Every morning, the balding man practically quivered when he brought in the daily news. Over the past week and half, the headlines had become more and more inflammatory.

"Has she seen any of these?" Andres asked.

"I'm not sure, Your Highness," Ronaldo replied, looking decidedly uncomfortable as he shifted from one foot to the other.

If she did, at least she couldn't read Spanish and wouldn't know the depth of the ugliness leveled at her.

"This is unacceptable. We will shut them down. Every one of the newspapers."

Ronaldo cleared his throat. "I understand your concerns, but—"

"My *concerns*?" He held up one of the papers. "These filthy rags are tearing her apart and showing blatant racism. They accuse her of "marrying up," allegedly the same way that her mother did. They accuse her and her mother of being adept at climbing the social ladder. And what about this one, that refers to her *exotic bloodline*? I want names. I want these so-called reporters brought up on charges and these goddamn newspapers shut down!" He shook with rage. He hadn't expected the attacks to have such racial undertones. What era were they in? The seventeen hundreds?

"Your Highness, do you mean to revoke the right to freedom of speech and eliminate freedom of the press? They have always been free to criticize the royal family. Is that no longer the case?"

He was used to negative comments in the press. Not everyone agreed with every decision the monarchy made, but this—this was downright abusive. Andres crumpled the paper in his hands and tossed it in the trash. He stalked aimlessly across the room to release the pent-up anger.

"You can ignore them or issue a strongly worded rebuke. While that is unprecedented, it will demonstrate that the palace does not condone these articles or what the television reporters have said. And they're not all bad. If you look inside that one"—Ronaldo pointed—"you'll see they think it's good that you're marrying a commoner and someone who doesn't have royal lineage. They think she'll be good for our country and shake things up from the norm. Get us away from centuries-old traditions and bring us into the twenty-first century."

All of the negativity could be damn near eliminated if his grandfather would give his approval of the marriage, but Andres hadn't been able to convince him to change his mind yet.

He rested his bottom on the edge of the desk. "I want a statement drawn up immediately. Before the end of the day because I want to send a clear message—*before the end of the day*—that these headlines, these articles, all of it, are nothing but harassment. Am I clear?"

"Yes, Your Highness. I will talk to the communications director right away." He scurried toward the door.

"And Ronaldo, make sure she doesn't see any of these. Is that understood? She doesn't speak Spanish yet, but she might be able to figure out what they're writing about her."

"Yes, Your Highness."

After Ronaldo left, Andres let out a worried breath. Was he doing the right thing? He felt he was, because he'd promised to protect Angela, and that's what he was doing. He found the articles troubling, but they would be extremely painful to her, and the last thing he wanted was for her to feel pain.

He only hoped he was making the right decision.

28

A ndres entered The Cream Room. Inside was dark because the heavy curtains on the windows were closed except for the one window that Angela sat in front of. The old chair had been moved into this room after his mother left. It was tan with ornate gold trim around the back of the seat. Angela sat ramrod straight as she stared out at the ocean. As Andres came closer, he noted the stack of magazines and newspapers on her lap, and his heart dropped.

Closing his eyes briefly, he wished for the right words to make whatever she was feeling go away. He continued forward on lead feet and dragged another chair catty corner to her. He sat down and watched her profile for a moment, not knowing what to say. He'd issued a strongly worded statement before the end of the day but didn't know if that was enough to fix the problem.

Angela turned to face him, and his heart wrenched when he saw her tear-streaked face. The cool calm he'd entered with was left frayed and tattered in the wake of the pain in her brown eyes. He couldn't fathom what she must be going through, and knowing he was the cause of it devastated him.

She tossed the magazines and newspapers to the floor. They

were all in English, and the headlines were much the same as the ones published in Estoria.

"You shouldn't read those," he said quietly.

"I shouldn't, but I guess I'm a glutton for punishment."

"I'll take care of it. I'll make them stop."

She gave a short laugh and looked away a spell before returning her gaze to him. Hurt swam in her eyes, and he wanted to gather her close and protect her. He reached for her, but she withdrew, her gaze accusatory.

"How? Some are quoting articles from Estoria, while others are simply stating what people in other countries think. Can you stop the press in every country, Andres? No, you can't." She swiped away the tears from her cheeks. "Is this what you wanted?"

"No," Andres replied in the same quiet voice.

"You sure? Because you don't seem to care about anyone or anything except what you want. This is the result of your need to have me and your child." She pointed at the periodicals on the floor. "This is the result of your need to force me to marry you."

The heat of shame burned his skin.

"I told you our relationship couldn't work. I can't do this, Andres. I love you, but I can't stay here and I can't marry you."

Panicked gripped his insides. "Angela—"

"I *won't*. And you can't make me."

"I will make this right. I love you."

"Don't. Don't say that," she said with an aggrieved expression, as if expressing his love caused her physical pain.

Their gazes locked, and silence filled the space between them.

Finally, Angela stood. She clasped her hands before her. "Your people don't want me."

Andres stood, as well. "They need time to get used to the idea."

"Do you really think I care? How could you think this would work? What kind of support are you prepared to give?"

"Whatever you need." How she could she doubt that he was ready and willing to give her anything and everything?

She shook her head. "Let me go, Andres."

"And if I can't?"

"You can do whatever you want, and that includes letting me go home. Don't make me stay where I'm not wanted. Your grandfather hasn't approved this marriage and you know as well as I do that he won't. Admit that it's over. We can't be together, and if you don't find a wife soon, Estoria risks losing its autonomy and going back to Portugal."

This time when he reached for her, she didn't withdraw, but she didn't put her arms around him like she always did. She stood stiff, but he pretended not to notice. One hand cupped the back of her head, and the other arm wound around her waist and held her close. "I need more time."

She shook her bowed head. "You want me to leave everything behind to be with you—my country, my job, my family—for you. I thought I could do it, but I can't. Not for this." Her voice thickened with tears and she looked at him with watery eyes. "What have you given up? What have *you* sacrificed? Nothing. Let me go, Andres. You can't have everything you want. It's time you learned that."

She stepped back and his arms fell away. For the first time he could remember, he hated his lot in life and hated that with all the power and money in his possession, he could not have the woman he most desired.

Neither of them spoke as all the hopelessness of their situation remained like a festering wound between them. There was so much Andres wanted to say, but there was no point in saying any of it. No point in telling her his mood shifted and changed with hers, the same way the moon controlled the rise and fall of the tide. Her pain was his pain. Her joy was his joy. Now his life would be emotionless and luster-less.

No point in explaining how much he loved and adored her and would do anything to make her happy. Because she was right. His grandfather hadn't given approval for them to marry, and without his approval, there were going to be more hurtful articles and inflammatory headlines. To put her through any more pain would be an act of selfishness he couldn't tolerate in himself.

He twisted the gold signet ring on his middle finger, engraved with the shield of the House of Vasquez. This life was not her destiny, it was his. His destiny had been set before he was even born.

"I will make arrangements for you to leave tomorrow."

Tears shimmered in her eyes. "Thank you."

He came to her and cradled her face in his hands. "I tried," he said thickly.

"I know," she said in a broken whisper.

Her lower lip trembled, and he pressed a soft kiss to her mouth.

"No matter who I marry, you will always be the love of my life."

She closed her eyes and a tear tracked down her left cheek. He brushed it away with his thumb and rested his forehead against hers.

"One of my aides will be in touch to make arrangements about...about the child." It pained him to have to say those words, to know that he would be a long-distance father to a child who he wanted to grow up under his supervision, love, and care.

Angela nodded her head in understanding, her lower lip trembling once again.

"Goodbye, *mi amor.*"

With one final glance at the dreaded periodicals scattered on the floor, he left the room. He took the long walk down the hall to his own bedroom. He'd spent most nights with Angela since her arrival, but he couldn't do it tonight. Not knowing that she'd leave him for good tomorrow.

He shut the door and walked in the dark to his bed. He thought about the lackluster future he had to look forward to, without Angela and the child who was a product of their love. He dropped onto the side of the bed.

He'd never known pain like this. His father's rejection and his mother's departure had hurt, but his grandfather's love had soothed the agony of losing both of his parents at such a young age. This pain felt like he was splitting in two, and no one could soothe him or diminish its effect. He didn't want anyone else.

Knees to elbows, he buried his face in his hands. He'd lost her again, and this time it was truly over.

Tonight was the lowest point of his life.

29

H e wasn't coming.

Standing at the open door of the limo in the private parking lot behind the palace, Angela searched the windows for a glimpse of Andres. She'd hoped to see him one last time, but he was nowhere to be found.

Though she'd suspected he wouldn't show, she'd nonetheless dallied in the hope that he'd make an appearance. But this was for the best, for both of them. A clean break. She'd spent most of the night crying, and she'd probably fall apart again if she saw him.

"Miss Lipscomb?" Ollie's voice drew her attention. "Did you forget something?" he asked gently.

"No. I have everything I came with." Except her heart, which would always belong to Andres. Her messenger bag and a few other personal items, however, were taking the flight with her back to Atlanta.

"It was a pleasure getting to know you, ma'am," Ollie said.

"It was a pleasure getting to know you, too," she said. "Do you mind if I give you a hug?"

He smiled. "Not at all."

She hugged him briefly.

"Take care, ma'am."

"You, too."

With a tremulous breath, Angela climbed into the back of the vehicle. Gustave closed the door, and within minutes she was on her way to the airport.

ANDRES CHECKED THE TIME, his attention shifting away from the instructions his grandfather was giving to him, Juan, and one of his aides. Angela had left a few days ago, and he was still numb. He hadn't called or sent a text. He'd had someone check up on her and knew she was staying at her parents' house for the time being. At least she wasn't alone.

He was fairly certain his grandfather had called this "emergency" meeting because he wanted to assess Andres's frame of mind but didn't want to be alone with him. They never held Monday meetings, and the topics Felipe covered could easily have been relayed between their personal secretaries. Maybe he was feeling guilty. Andres couldn't be sure. He'd told his grandfather he let Angela go home, and though he hadn't expressed any joy, it was clear that he thought Andres had made the right decision.

Agitated, he ran shaky fingers through his hair and refocused on the conversation.

Felipe came to sit behind his desk. "I think we have everything handled. Juan, you will attend the meetings in Australia and represent the family at the wedding in Istanbul."

"Yes, and when the Italian president comes on vacation, I'll meet with him and arrange activities for him and his wife to participate in," Juan added.

He's so eager to please, Andres thought. Felipe didn't see Juan as worthy of the throne, but he worked hard, and his heart was in the right place. He loved his country and believed in upholding traditions—traditions that Andres found stifling and outdated.

Felipe looked at him, a hint of worry in his eyes not conveyed when he spoke with his usual authoritative voice. "Andres, you will be responsible for giving out the biannual innovators' awards, starting next year."

The awards were the brainchild of Felipe for a program he instituted after taking the throne years ago. Plaques were given out in a number of categories to those who made strides in science, technology, and medicine.

"I will also have you—"

"No." Andres suddenly felt very tired. Tired of pretending he was happy and tired of pretending he had any interest in this farcical meeting.

The aide, Juan and Felipe stared at him.

"Excuse me?" Felipe said.

He'd had to choose—his heart or the throne, and he'd made the wrong choice. He suddenly knew what he had to do. He had to walk away. He had to give up the throne.

Why hadn't he thought of that before? His grandfather had chosen him as next in line, but he didn't have to accept. With his inheritance and the revenue from his private equity firm, he could provide a very comfortable life for himself, Angela, and their future children, all without his princely responsibilities.

His decision would initially create a sensation in the press and an upheaval in the country, so he'd have to wait a while before he and Angela could be together, to protect her from the backlash. But it could be done. It absolutely could be done.

Andres stood, emboldened by his decision, heart racing faster —not with fear, but with excitement. Holding his head high, he said, "I love Angela, Grandfather, and if tradition dictates that I can't be with the woman I love, then I no longer want to be a part of this life."

The aide gasped, Juan's mouth fell open, and Felipe jumped to his feet.

"Absolutely not!" Felipe yelled.

"Your Serene Highness, I hereby renounce my right to the throne of Estoria and abdicate my position to Juan the Viscount of Guzman."

The aide gasped again and Juan's mouth fell open even wider.

"Get out!" Felipe kept his eyes on Andres but spoke to the other two men with the point of his finger.

The aide jumped to his feet and exited immediately, but Juan remained seated, clearly stunned as he continued to stare at Andres.

Andres lifted his head defiantly. "With your guidance, Juan can handle my duties. He will also have the National Council to turn to for advice."

"I asked you to leave," Felipe seethed through gritted teeth.

Juan scrambled to his feet and rushed out the door.

When they were alone, his grandfather glowered at him with a mixture of disbelief and anger. "Now I know you have clearly lost your mind. You would give up the crown for this woman?"

"Yes." All he could think about were her eyes—first trusting and believing in him, and then filled with tears as they reflected her anguish. He'd failed her and disappointed himself.

"Think about what you're doing. This country cannot survive without you."

"And I cannot survive without her."

"What about Estoria? How could you cast aside your duty, your love of country, for the love of a woman? I would never do such a thing. That's not how I raised you."

"You raised me to think for myself and not to blindly follow anyone's lead, including yours. You chose duty over love. I choose love over duty. I won't change my mind, Grandfather. This is the right decision."

"You know I'm not well. If you don't take the throne, we risk being annexed back to Portugal. All our assets, everything will belong to another country."

"Juan can take my place."

"He is not ready. He does not have your judgment, and I've already made the announcement that *you* will succeed me."

Felipe trembled with emotion, and for a moment, Andres was torn. He'd started to look forward to leading his country as a prince with modern ideas, bringing the nation into the twenty-first century and slowly eliminating traditions that no longer made sense. Further, he didn't want to disappoint his grandfather, and he worried about the direction the country would take under Juan's leadership. But he couldn't live the rest of his life according to someone else's terms. He couldn't allow his child to grow up without him, and he couldn't spend the rest of his days without the woman he loved.

"We can put off the announcement to a more appropriate time, but my decision is made. Juan is already married, and we have eight months to get him ready."

"You're making a terrible mistake," Felipe said.

Andres smiled. Despite his grandfather's love, he'd always felt abandoned by both his parents. His father hadn't wanted him, and his mother hadn't fought to take him with her. She'd left and started a new life with a new family. He didn't want his own child to experience those feelings of neglect and abandonment, nor did he want to wake up next to anyone else but Angela Lipscomb.

"No. My mistake was letting her go. I will make sure my affairs are in order so that the transition is smooth for Juan." He turned on his heel, contemplating what must be done, and thinking about how soon he'd be able to see Angela again.

"If you do this, you not only turn your back on your country, you turn your back on me. There is no coming back, Andres!" Felipe called after him.

The threat didn't slow his steps out the door. He was ready to do what he hadn't been able to do before.

Sacrifice for love.

30

While a cold November rain pelted the windows outside, Angela lay wrapped in a blanket on the sofa watching television with her parents. Martin sat in his recliner, and Tessa at the opposite end of the sofa with Angela's sock-covered feet in her lap.

She'd been back in the States for a week and had no interest in going back to work for the time being. She hid at her parents' house, letting them baby her as she recovered from her emotional wounds. Night after night, sleep eluded her, and when she finally did get some rest, a few hours later it was interrupted when she woke up weeping. She'd cried so much she should be dehydrated.

She firmly believed that in walking away she'd done the right thing. The ugly words in those articles twisted like a familiar knife that had regained its sharpness. Yet, there were moments when she wished she could have been stronger and stayed with Andres. If his grandfather had given his approval, she could have stuck it out, knowing they had his support.

She didn't want to think about what Andres was doing now, but her mind constantly strayed to him. She imagined he'd already resumed the search for a wife. Unlike last time they were apart, she didn't go online to find out news about him. She was determined to separate her life from his, go cold turkey, until she heard from one of his aides about how he wanted to handle matters like visitation and education for the baby.

Certain he'd want to be present for their child's birth, she hoped she could keep her emotions in check when he arrived. She placed a hand on her stomach and smiled. She didn't get to marry a prince, the man she loved, but they'd created a life together, and she could celebrate that, at least.

The doorbell chimed, and her mother glanced at her father. "Were you expecting company?" she asked.

"No. Were you, Angela?" Martin asked.

"No," she replied.

"Who could possibly be here at this time of night? I'll see who it is." Martin stood up with a groan and shuffled out of the room.

Moments later, Angela heard muffled male voices at the front but couldn't tell what anyone was saying.

"Um, Angela," her father called. There was an odd sound to his voice. "I need you to come here right now, honey."

She sat up and frowned at her mother. Tessa shrugged.

Angela stood and dropped the blanket and quickly smoothed her messy hair. She and her mother went down the hall toward the front door. When they entered the foyer, she couldn't believe her eyes.

Standing right outside the door was Prince Felipe. She'd never seen him in person but recognized him from photos. He looked distinguished with his gray hair and gray goatee, and a dark suit and gloves. Two men in suits stood on either side of him getting pelted by the rain, while one of them held a large black umbrella over the prince's head.

In addition to the two men, six additional security guards were behind them, more than she'd ever seen Andres travel with. Then there were four dark vehicles parked at the curb—a limo and three SUVs, all with tinted windows.

Her father glanced back at her with a silent question on his face.

Angela walked slowly toward Prince Felipe and managed to find her voice. "Prince Felipe, what are you doing here?"

"Is there somewhere we can talk privately?"

"Yes, of course. Please, come in."

She and her father stepped aside and the prince entered, carefully wiping his feet on the mat at the door. His eyes did a quick scan of the interior. For most people, their house, built with the proceeds of a very successful career in the music industry, was grand by any standard. But she couldn't help but wonder what a prince who was used to living in a palace built hundreds of years ago thought.

The two guards followed him in and stood inside at the closed front door.

"You can use the sitting room," Tessa said. She pointed to the first room off to the right. "Would you like something to drink? Lemonade or..." Clearly flustered, her hands moved aimlessly.

"No, I'm fine, thank you," Prince Felipe said with a smile.

Tessa patted her hair nervously, and Martin moved to stand beside her. He took her arm by the elbow. "We'll leave you two alone to talk." He shot another curious glance at Angela and then shuffled his wife down the hallway.

In the sitting room, Prince Felipe sat in an armchair, and Angela sat on the edge of the loveseat facing him. Having him show up unexpectedly to her parents' house on a Friday night not only made her nervous but made her wonder why he'd made the trip. For a split second she wondered if something had happened to Andres but scolded her inner negative voice and waited for him to explain his visit.

"I'm sure you're wondering why I am here," he said. His voice was deep, cultured, and accented like Andres's.

"Yes, I am."

"Has Andres told you about my...medical situation?"

"Yes, he has. He explained that's why he had to ascend to the throne next year," Angela said carefully.

"That is correct. We haven't made my diagnosis public yet, but behind the scenes we are making ready for when I can no longer rule. Part of that preparation involved installing my successor sooner rather than later. My son should have succeeded me, but because he is not able to rule, I have the right to choose my own successor, and I chose Andres. I believe he would have gladly accepted his new role if not for you."

Angela bristled, uncertain of the direction the conversation was about to take.

"My grandson is very much in love with you. In fact, I've never seen him like this." He paused. "Have you heard from him since you left?"

"No, I haven't."

"Well, what I'm about to say may surprise you. It certainly did me. Because of his love for you, Andres has refused to ascend to the throne."

"Wh-what?"

"He will walk away from everything he knows, his destiny, from me. I've spent the last few days trying to convince him otherwise, but he won't be moved, and time is of the essence." He lapsed into the story of how Andres announced his decision to abdicate.

"I can't believe he would do that," Angela said when he finished.

"He has. Now I have a question for you. Do you love my grandson?"

"With all my heart," Angela said without hesitation.

"Then come back to Estoria and marry him. I will give my blessing, which should take care of much of the opposition you encountered when you first arrived. There is also something about a royal wedding that recharges the people and makes them optimistic about the future."

Angela hesitated. "I-I don't know if I can do that."

"You said you love my grandson, is that correct?"

"Yes, I do," she assured him.

His face hardened as he looked at her, and his body angled

toward hers. "Then come back with me. If you return, I know Andres will accept his role. Your decision will alter the course of history. The fate of an entire nation rests on your shoulders. If you don't marry him, he'll walk away from us—his family, his country, his destiny. I am asking not as a prince, but as a man who knows what my grandson is capable of. I know he is the right person for the throne. If I give my blessing, will you return? And will you convince him to stay?"

31

A ngela figured one day she'd be back on Estorian soil—
one day, but not so soon. Yet here she was, having taken
a transatlantic flight with Prince Felipe on the Royal
Plane of Estoria.

After her conversation with him, she had asked for twenty-four
hours because she was nervous and didn't want to make a hasty
decision based on emotion. She loved Andres and knew he loved
her, but if she was going to have a life with him, she wanted to be
sure that she was emotionally ready to do so. After a lengthy
conversation with her parents, she made her decision and slept on
it. The next morning she called Prince Felipe at his hotel and
agreed to travel back to Estoria with him.

This time, she was better prepared for the trip. She packed her
clothes and other necessities and hugged her parents goodbye
with tear-filled eyes.

She convinced Prince Felipe not to call ahead and let Andres
know she was coming. By the time their motorcade arrived in the
private parking lot at the back of the Royal Palace of Estoria, night
had fallen.

One of the servants took her luggage to The Cream Room
where she had stayed before, and then she made her way to

Andres's bedroom. Instead of knocking, she eased open the door and quietly walked in. Lamps cast light in the room, which was decorated in a contemporary pallet of slate gray, white, and cream. The bed she'd slept in with him a couple of times looked large enough to accommodate ten people. The first time she saw it, she'd teased him about having orgies there, which he'd vehemently denied.

She heard the shower and smiled, thinking she should surprise him in the bathroom. This scenario reminded her of another time when he showed up unexpectedly at her house and waited for her to come out of the bathroom. She decided to do the same.

She removed her shoes and climbed onto the bed to wait. She didn't have to wait long. A few minutes later, Andres exited the bathroom with a towel wrapped around his lean waist, his firm muscular chest exposed, and his hair damp with water.

His beauty and presence took her breath away. God she loved this man! To think she'd given him up.

He paused and did a double take. He stared, frowned, then ran a hand down his face as if he thought he had imagined her.

"I'm not a figment of your imagination. I'm really here," Angela said.

Unable to wait any longer, she slid from the bed and rushed over to him. He pulled her up into his arms, lifting her off the floor. She wrapped her legs around his waist and hugged him tight.

He continued to stare at her, his expression halfway between surprise and wonderment. "What are you doing here? How did you...?"

"Your grandfather. He came to see me in Atlanta and told me what you did. I can't believe you would give up all of this for me." She kissed him and kissed him again. She'd missed his mouth, his skin, his smell.

Andres strolled over to the bed and sat down with her straddling his lap. His brow wrinkled in confusion. "I knew he had taken a trip, but his staff was very hush-hush about where he was going. To be quite honest, I've been pre-occupied and didn't push.

I assumed his trip had something to do with his treatment for Alzheimer's. Maybe he was looking into an experimental procedure, which he'd told me he was open to." He cupped her face. "I can't believe this. Are you saying he will give his permission for us to marry?"

"Yes."

"Why didn't he tell me you were coming?"

"I asked him not to."

She explained the chain of events, from the time Prince Felipe showed up at her parents' house, to her arrival with him tonight.

"I can't let you give up your title. I love you, Andres. The fact that you'd be willing to do that for me…" Her voice cracked. "I'll marry you." She kissed him and brushed away that unruly curl that always fell across his brow. She reveled in the gentle pressure of his mouth. "I'll marry you."

Smoothing his hand down her loose hair, he looked directly into her eyes. "I never wanted to sacrifice anything until you. Nothing matters without you. But are you sure this is what you want? My grandfather can be very convincing."

She laughed, giddy. Ecstatic. Ready to face whatever came her way with this man at her side. "He did mention something about altering the course of history."

"*Hala.*" Andres shook his head and studied her. "You're not back here because of guilt, are you? I want to be with you. I want to raise a family with you. We can do that anywhere, without the trappings of titles and royal protocol. You don't have to be a part of my crazy world."

She held his hand. "I know I have a lot to learn, but I'm ready to be a part of it, as long as you're in it. Prince Felipe thinks that once he gives his approval and the palace issues an engagement announcement, that will eliminate the negativity."

"*Some* of the negativity, not all." His eyes saddened. "Perhaps I was naïve, but the attacks you received were uncalled for and disappointing. To know that my own people feel that way was… eye-opening."

"But it's not everyone," Angela said gently. She squeezed his hand. "Let's not give negative, hateful people so much power that they keep you from your rightful place in history. I love you, Andres. I love you more than I ever thought I was capable of loving anyone. I'll stand by your side and work with you as much as you need me to. And every now and again, I'll just need you to hold my hand."

"*Ay, te quiero mucho, mi amor,*" he whispered with a smile. He trailed soft kisses down the side of her face and along her throat. "I will hold your hand. I will hold your ass. I will hold your—"

"Stop!" Angela slapped his chest and burst into a fit of giggles.

Andres chuckled softly, laughing into her skin. She wrapped her arms around his neck as he rolled her onto her back. He gazed down into her eyes, and she trailed her fingers through his damp hair.

"You're really here," he said.

"Yes, I'm here."

"*Ay Dios, te quiero mucho.*"

He kissed her again, and slowly they made love until he entered her with one smooth stroke and a moan spilled with urgency from her lips. His thrusting hips took them over the edge into an intense, emotional climax that left them clinging to each other for a long time afterward.

32

"You look beautiful, baby," Tessa said.

"Thank you, Mom." Today was her wedding day, and her mother had arrived a few days ago to help.

Angela stood up from the couch. Despite the nervous flutter in her belly, she was ready to be Andres's wife.

The dress she wore had embroidered flowers decorating the bodice and climbing from the hemline halfway up the A-line skirt. The voluminous tulle skirt hid her four-month pregnancy bump, and a sweetheart neckline with capped off-the-shoulder sleeves tastefully showed off her shape and bare arms. Her makeup was simple, and so was her jewelry. She only wore diamond earrings, a gift from Prince Felipe, and used the natural waves in her hair to advantage to create a full, elegant updo.

As was customary in Estorian royal weddings, there were no bridesmaids or groomsmen. However, a very pregnant Dahlia had flown in from Zamibia to provide moral support, with a full medical staff in case she went into labor. During the past few weeks, their conversations had been invaluable in getting Angela's mind right as she went through the adjustment of becoming a member of the royal family. In addition, six attendants, two professional makeup artists, and hairdressers helped in the preparations.

As promised, Prince Felipe had proclaimed his approval of the wedding and a formal announcement had been made to introduce Angela to the local as well as international press. All of the negative articles did not go away, but with the full force of Prince Felipe and the palace's communications team, a more positive narrative around the couple's engagement became the norm, particularly when reporters learned that their whirlwind courtship had started at another royal wedding. Some deemed their meeting as destiny, but no matter the point of view, a certain excitement was generated throughout the island nation, reinvigorating the monarchy.

One of the attendants approached, a middle-aged woman with dark hair pulled back into a chignon. "Should I tell them we're ready?" she asked.

Angela nodded. "Yes. Tell them we're ready."

The woman left the room and the other attendants followed.

Tessa approached and held her hands. She stood back and took a good look at her. "I'm so proud of you and the strength you exhibited in the face of so much negativity. I've always wanted to protect you from anything that was bad, but I realize now that's not the best way. There was no need to coddle you, and you can fight for yourself. You've made both me and your father proud."

Angela's eyes grew misty. "Thank you, Mom."

They hugged briefly and then Dahlia approached.

"Who knew that in less than a year we would be attending another wedding—another royal wedding at that."

Angela laughed. "Thank you so much for being there for me and being a sounding board."

"Well, we still have a lot of work to do, but we'll figure out this life together. See you in the church."

They hugged, getting as close as they could with Dahlia's belly protruding between them, and then Dahlia and her mother left, leaving Angela alone.

She entwined her fingers together and wondered what Andres was doing now. Was he also nervous, or confident and calm?

She paced over to the window and looked out beyond the front courtyard to the throng of people lining the streets. News cameras and reporters from the United States and all over Europe and the world were present to capture her trip from the palace grounds to the oldest church in Estoria, established by Andres's ancestors during the founding of the country.

She took another breath and touched her stomach. She looked forward to the days when her waist would expand and she could fully enjoy being pregnant.

There was a knock on the door, and Angela turned away from the window. "Come in," she called.

The brunette attendant stepped inside. "Your carriage awaits," she said with a smile.

She affixed Angela's veil and with her assistance and that of another attendant, Angela made her way down the steps to the horse-drawn carriage. The women carefully folded in her train and closed the door. From there to the church she would have to ride alone.

The coachman clicked his tongue, and the horses took off at a trot. They traveled along the streets lined with spectators waving the flag of Estoria and cheering as she passed by. Angela waved at the onlookers, their excitement rubbing off on her and diminishing the fit of nerves that kept her from eating a bite all morning long.

The carriage ride took them to the front of the church where more attendants helped her down. They adjusted the train and held it off the ground as Angela started walking, cameras flashing all around. She briefly acknowledged them with a faint smile but remained focused and walked carefully up the three steps into the vestibule where her father waited with tears in his eyes.

Arm in arm they waited for the signal from the organist.

"You look lovely. I'm so happy I'm alive to see this day," Martin whispered. "Does this Prince Andres guy know how lucky he is?"

Angela blinked rapidly and glanced up at him. "I believe he does, but if he doesn't, I'll make sure to remind him."

They grinned at each other.

Soon, the beginning strains of the Estorian wedding march

sounded. Uniformed male attendants took their time opening the large golden doors and stepped aside.

Bouquet in hand, Angela walked down the aisle on her father's arm. She kept her gaze trained on Andres, who wore a dark suit with a red House of Vasquez sash across his torso.

With a broken sob, Martin handed her over to Andres. Angela squeezed his arm and her father turned quickly away and hurried to where Tessa sat.

She took a deep breath and faced her future husband.

As Andres lifted the veil, she noted that his eyes were a bright blue—brighter than she'd ever seen them. "*Te quiero,*" he mouthed to her.

"*Te quiero, tambien,*" she mouthed back.

EPILOGUE

The Red Room in the Royal Palace of Estoria was filled with period furniture made with rich, vibrant fabrics. The House of Vasquez used the room to receive foreign dignitaries and as a location for important announcements. None was more important than the one Prince Felipe would make today.

Andres stood solemnly beside his grandfather, directly across the room from a group of photographers and video cameras that would send out a live broadcast of Prince Felipe's abdication speech. Angela stood off to his left with other members of the royal family positioned around the room, including Juan the Viscount of Guzman. Juan's features remained stoic, but less than an hour before he'd worn a surly expression, still smarting from the fact that Andres had not walked away from the throne as promised. His cousin may never forgive him.

"We are ready, Your Highness," the palace communications director said. He crossed his hands in front of him and stood behind one of the cameras, next to the cameraman, awaiting Prince Felipe's signal.

The old man took a step forward and straightened his spine. A staff member handed him the speech. He stood very still and cleared his throat. "I am ready."

The light on the camera came on. Prince Felipe issued a brief greeting and then launched into his speech.

"...last year my decision to renounce the throne did not come easy. This very serious decision has made my heart heavy, but I made up my mind to do so in the best interest of our country. The burden of responsibility has become too much for me to bear, but the decision to relinquish that responsibility has been less difficult with the knowledge that my successor, whose training and fine qualities are of the highest caliber, is more than capable to pick up the mantle.

"Today I discharged my last duty as prince and reigning monarch, succeeded by my grandson, Prince Andres Luis Vasquez Alamanzar II. From this day forward I declare my allegiance to him, with all my heart and with no reservations.

"We have a new ruler. I wish wisdom, happiness, and God's blessings on his rule. God save the Prince of Estoria!"

"God save the Prince of Estoria!" everyone in the room repeated.

Prince Felipe took the red sash from an aide, and the two of them placed it on Andres's shoulder and secured it at his hip, indicating the transfer of power. Then Felipe bowed his head in respect.

Andres nodded and then stood next his grandfather. As cameras captured the aftermath, his eyes gravitated to Angela.

She was serene, a faint smile on her face.

Tonight and tomorrow there would be celebrations all over the island, ending with a formal reception and dinner tomorrow night. During all the activities, she would be right by his side.

SEATED ON THE BED, Angela watched her two-month-old daughter's brown eyes flutter closed as she rocked her in her arms. She and Andres were due to go downstairs to the formal dinner, but Elena Cristina had been fussy tonight, and she simply couldn't walk away with her baby's whimpering cries on her mind. The nanny hovered nearby and so did two attendants waiting to help Angela finish getting dressed, who'd tutted their concern that she'd soil her cream gown.

Andres entered the room. He was fully dressed in a tuxedo and the ceremonial red sash angled across his torso. "We have to go. They're waiting," he said in Spanish.

"I know," she said reluctantly, also in Spanish. After living in Estoria for almost a year and intensive lessons from a no-nonsense tutor, her language skills had vastly improved.

Andres sat down beside her. "She'll be fine." He smoothed a hand over Cristina's hair and dropped a kiss to her forehead.

Angela knew he hated to leave, too, but he was much better at adhering to duty than she was. Some days she still struggled with balancing their personal life with their public responsibilities, but it was getting easier.

She signaled to the nanny, who came over and took the baby out of the room, and Angela stood. One of the attendants quickly came over and lowered in front of her. She removed Angela's slippers and placed gold heels on her feet. The other attendant placed the tiara on her head and secured it into her up do. Now all that was left was the jewelry. Her arms would remain bare, but she was going to wear gold pieces from the royal collection around her neck and in her ears.

One attendant fastened a chunky gold necklace with a large gold pendant around her neck, while the other placed the matching dangling earrings in her ears. The solid gold necklace was heavy. The earrings were heavy, too, but the hollowed-out center decreased the strain on her earlobes.

Angela checked her appearance in a wall mirror. The jewelry definitely enhanced the off-the-shoulder dress. She turned to face Andres. "Well, what do you think?"

A wolfish grin took over his lips.

"Don't you dare," she said, shooting him a warning look.

"What?" Andres said with mock innocence. He walked over

and took her hand. "I was only going to say that you look beauti-ful. Doesn't my wife look beautiful?" he asked the other two women.

"Yes, she does," they agreed.

As she'd suspected, he wasn't done. He leaned down to her ear and lapsed into English. "And I cannot wait until the end of this dinner so I can have my way with you, *mi amor*."

Blushing, Angela grinned and shook her head. He was incorri-gible, and she loved him to death.

With Andres leading the way, they took the stairs to the first floor and walked to the banquet hall. Two footmen stood outside the closed double doors. On Andres's signal, they opened the doors and the couple stepped over the threshold.

Over one hundred attendees filled the tables. Cameras flashed, and everyone seated came to their feet and bowed or curtsied.

A male staff member standing off to the side in evening dress and a very stiff posture made the formal announcement. "Good evening! I present to you His Serene Highness, Prince Andres Luis Vasquez Alamanzar II and Her Royal Highness, Princess Angela Renee Lipscomb de Vasquez."

Then Andres and Angela walked in to greet their guests.

Excerpt: Princess of Zamibia

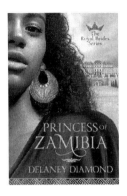

Travel to the fictional country of Zamibia in West Africa, in *Princess of Zamibia* (Royal Brides #1), and experience the royal romance between Dahlia Sommers and Crown Prince Kofi Francois Karunzika, Conquering Lion of the tribe of Mbutu.

～

Kofi settled his gaze on Dahlia as she walked slowly down the sidewalk with a toddler in her arms, bundled against the unusually cold night. She wore a green knit cap pulled low on her head to protect her ears. Dark hair styled in two thick braids peeked from beneath the knit cap to land past her shoulder blades. The child was wrapped just as warmly as she, his head resting on her shoulder as he appeared to sleep.

As she neared, Kofi's stomach tightened and his nostrils flared —an instinctive response to seeing the woman at whose feet he'd once planned to place the world. He couldn't quite see her lush lips from this distance, but he remembered their taste and how she'd trembled beneath him—his harsh breaths melting with her soft pants. His body tightened, every muscle tense. He could almost hear her breathless cries, feel her undulating hips as he drove into her with frenzied thrusts.

Against his volition, his heart rate accelerated, pumping hot blood through his veins. After three years he still couldn't control his body's immediate reaction to seeing her. He clenched his fists to fight the involuntary acknowledgment and swallowed the bitter taste of betrayal. He'd never wanted a woman the way he had wanted Dahlia Sommers. Never needed one as much. And that had been his mistake.

His gaze shifted to the child, and he leaned forward, anxious to get a good look as they came into the light spilling from the front door of the building, but the child's face was hidden from view. He'd hoped to catch an in-person glimpse of the son he found out existed only days ago. Once the private investigator told him and sent the damning photos of a toddler who looked almost identical to him at the same age, he dropped everything as quickly as he could and traveled to the United States.

His eyes narrowed on the mother of his child as her feet hesitated at the bottom of the steps. She looked up the street. For a moment he thought she saw him in the SUV, but then she turned and hurried into the building, clutching the child protectively in her arms. Almost as if she sensed his presence and knew why he came.

Kofi's jaw firmed as he sat back in the leather seat and rested a wrist on his knee. He would wait until she was settled in her apartment, and then he would go up. No rush. He'd found her and knew the truth. And with the truth came the only option for action available.

He would take his son, next in line to the throne of Zamibia. He would not leave the country without him.

ALSO BY DELANEY DIAMOND

Quicksand

- A Powerful Attraction
- Without You

Royal Brides

- Princess of Zamibia
- Princess of Estoria
- Queen of Barrakesch (coming in 2020)

Brooks Family series

- Passion Rekindled
- Do Over
- Wild Thoughts

Love Unexpected series

- The Blind Date
- The Wrong Man
- An Unexpected Attraction
- The Right Time
- One of the Guys
- That Time in Venice

Johnson Family series

- Unforgettable
- Perfect
- Just Friends

- The Rules
- Good Behavior

Latin Men series

- The Arrangement
- Fight for Love
- Private Acts
- The Ultimate Merger
- Second Chances
- More Than a Mistress
- Undeniable
- Hot Latin Men: Vol. I (print anthology)
- Hot Latin Men: Vol. II (print anthology)

Hawthorne Family series

- The Temptation of a Good Man
- A Hard Man to Love
- Here Comes Trouble
- For Better or Worse
- Hawthorne Family Series: Vol. I (print anthology)
- Hawthorne Family Series: Vol. II (print anthology)

Bailar series (sweet/clean romance)

- Worth Waiting For

Stand Alones

- A Passionate Love
- Still in Love
- Subordinate Position
- Heartbreak in Rio

Other

- Audiobooks
- Free Stories

ABOUT THE AUTHOR

Delaney Diamond is the USA Today Bestselling Author of sweet, sensual, passionate romance novels. Originally from the U.S. Virgin Islands, she now lives in Atlanta, Georgia. She reads romance novels, mysteries, thrillers, and a fair amount of nonfiction. When she's not busy reading or writing, she's in the kitchen trying out new recipes, dining at one of her favorite restaurants, or traveling to an interesting locale.

Enjoy free reads and the first chapter of all her novels on her website. Join her mailing list to get sneak peeks, notices of sale prices, and find out about new releases.

Join her mailing list
www.delaneydiamond.com

facebook.com/DelaneyDiamond
twitter.com/DelaneyDiamond
pinterest.com/DelaneyDiamond
instagram.com/authordelaneydiamond

Made in the USA
Columbia, SC
16 April 2019